The First Urban Farm Fresh Romance

Secrets of Sunbeams

Print ISBN: 9781988068145
E-Book ISBN: 9781988068121

This is a work of fiction set in a redrawn Spokane, Washington. Businesses and locations are used fictitiously. Any resemblance to actual persons, living or dead, is coincidental.

First edition, GreenWords Media, 2016

THE FIRST URBAN FARM FRESH ROMANCE

Secrets of Sunbeams

VALERIE COMER

Dedication

For Barb

Acknowledgments

This has been a fun story to write! If you're familiar with Spokane, Washington, you may (sort of) recognize the "Bridgeview" neighborhood... with adaptations. Also, the animal control division does not work out of the city office any more as I've portrayed in this story, but from a county office in nearby Spokane Valley. I definitely took some liberties for the sake of the story on several counts, which I hope you'll forgive.

Secrets of Sunbeams first released as part of a limited-time, multi-author e-book box set, Whispers of Love, which you probably won't find for sale anymore. I mention it because I'm so thankful to the other eleven authors for including me in what became a USA Today bestselling set! We debuted at #79 after much hard work. Thank you to Jan Thompson for her hard work in setting up the set, and to my fellow authors: Kimberly Rae Jordan, Leah Atwood, Sally Bradley, Christina Coryell, JoAnn Durgin, Autumn Macarthur, Lesley Ann McDaniel, Carol Moncado, Staci Stallings, and Marion Ueckermann.

Thanks to Tina, Jacqui, and Gretchen for having a great eye for detail as beta readers, and also to my entire street team for cheering me on throughout the process and helping fine-tune the story description. You ladies are so appreciated every day!

As ever, hugs and thanks to Nicole, without whom I wouldn't have half the success I do today. You rock as both a friend and an editor.

I'm thankful every day for my fellow inspirational romance author friends at www.inspyromance.com and my Christian Indie Authors group. Thanks to you all for walking the journey with me both personally and professionally.

I wish I could tell you that Global Sunbeams is a real company, or that there was a mission dedicated to getting solar to Africa, but there isn't that I know of. Samaritan's Purse does, however, offer goats and other animals to villagers in various parts of Africa.

Thanks to Marianne, Jake, and Rachel for providing modeling for the cover (goats in the first case, people in the other cases!) and to Hanna of Book Cover Bakery for pulling together yet another delightful romance cover.

Thanks to the many readers who've emailed, sharing their excitement to shift from their beloved Farm Fresh Romance series to the new urbanized version. I couldn't do it without all of you!

Thanks to my husband, Jim, for research trips to Spokane and talking through scenarios — to say nothing of everyday love and support — and to my kids and grandgirls for cheering me on and embracing the idiosyncrasies of having an author for a mom and grandmother.

And my deepest gratitude goes to Jesus, without whom I would not have stories to tell. If there is any secret to my sunshine, let me point to Him, the source of all light and life.

Books by Valerie Comer

Farm Fresh Romance Novels

Raspberries and Vinegar
Wild Mint Tea
Sweetened with Honey
Dandelions for Dinner
Plum Upside Down
Berry on Top

Riverbend Romance Novellas

Secretly Yours
Pinky Promise
Sweet Serenade
Team Bride
Merry Kisses

Urban Farm Fresh Romance Novels

Secrets of Sunbeams
Butterflies on Breezes
Memories of Mist

Christmas in Montana Romance Series

More Than a Tiara
Other Than a Halo

Chapter 1

EDEN ANDRUSEK STOPPED so suddenly the screen door slammed her backside. Where was Pansy? Eden shaded her eyes and glanced around the backyard. No way. She'd only been inside a minute.

"Pansy!" she yelled, jogging down the three steps to the barren yard. "Where are you?"

The answer seemed to be nowhere. Eden's gut clenched. No, no. No, no, no. This can't be happening.

The gate at the side of the small house was definitely closed. The backyard was completely fenced with no hiding places. Except...

Eden's pulse quickened at the sight of a vertical board in the side fence hanging slightly askew. She ran across the yard, stumbling over the metal bucket Pansy had been playing with, and pushed at the errant board. It swung aside. That was definitely enough room for the escape artist.

She crouched and peered through the gap into the neatly mowed lawn of the Victorian next door. A side table with a glass of something clear and red sat beside an empty deck chair facing—

"Pansy! No."

The goat only glanced over as she chewed the paper dangling from her mouth.

"Drop it, Pansy." Like that would help. Dogs might be trainable. Goats? Not so much. Eden yanked at the board, but she wasn't as skinny as the Nigerian dwarf. No way was she fitting through that gap. And she definitely wasn't going over the eight-foot fence without a ladder.

Eden dropped the board and bolted through her gate and around to the house next door. Man, they didn't even have a side gate. She pounded on the door while jabbing the doorbell. Wasn't there a new renter? Surely someone was home. Somebody had to have left the nearly full glass out there, to say nothing of the papers.

The papers that were being devoured in present time.

She pounded again. "Let me in!"

No voice. No footsteps.

Eden twisted the doorknob, and it gave beneath her fingers. She hesitated for an instant. Should she do this? Was it breaking in if the door was unlocked? Maybe she should go back to her yard, grab a hammer and remove another board or two. That had to be better than entering someone's house uninvited.

She pushed just a little further. Was there a clear path to the back door from here? Maybe she could scoot through with no one the wiser. After all, if someone were home, they'd surely have come to the door by now.

A set of patio doors was clearly visible past the dimly lit interior. On the other side, Pansy knocked the glass onto the deck chair and began to lap up the liquid.

"Hello?" called Eden, gaze locked on Pansy.

"Hey!" a male voice exploded. "Get out of my yard."

A guy Eden had never seen before wrenched the glass door open and ran onto the patio, his tanned arms flailing.

Whoa. No wonder they called those things muscle shirts. She shouldn't be staring, but she couldn't help herself as he grabbed the remains of the papers off the side table and began to whack Pansy with them.

That did it. No one was going to smack Pansy but her. Not that the goat didn't deserve it. Eden dashed through the house and out onto the back deck, skidding to a stop beside them.

"Don't hit her. That's my goat."

The guy pivoted, hand still holding the sheaf of paper high in the air. His blue eyes blazed at her from beneath damp, disheveled blond curls that stuck out all over, like he'd been toweling it dry when duty called. "Who are you?"

He was cute. Eden gulped. He was also stinkin' angry, and he had a right to be. She grabbed Pansy's halter and wrenched the slobbery paper fragments from the goat's mouth. She closed her eyes for one brief moment, then straightened and looked her new neighbor in the eye. Although his eyes were much higher than hers.

"My name is Eden Andrusek, and this is Pansy. We, um, we live next door." She pointed. "She broke through the fence. I'm really sorry. I—" she hesitated, glancing at the remaining papers "—I hope this wasn't anything important."

His eyebrows shot up. "Sorry is a good start, but your hope is misguided." He smacked the sheaf against the table, and Eden jumped. He scrubbed a palm against his forehead and shook his head. "You have no idea."

"Is there anything I can do to help?" Eden ventured. She

glanced at an architectural drawing on the top page. “Maybe not.”

“All you can do is get that stupid animal out of here and fix your fence. I should call the City of Spokane animal control on you.”

“They’re already here,” she mumbled.

“They’re what?”

“That’s my job.” Not likely something she should admit to, as angry as he seemed. Eden dragged Pansy back a step. “Please don’t call my boss. It won’t happen again. I’ll fix that board and check all the other ones, too. I promise.”

“You’re serious.” He took a deep breath and let it out slowly. “I don’t know how I’ll get this report done before the meeting on Tuesday now.”

“I’m really sorry.” Which, of course, didn’t help.

He flipped through the papers and chewed on his bottom lip. “Some of it I can reprint. But some were longhand notes to go with the sketches I was doodling. I’d just figured out how to mount the panels on the peaked roof.”

Eden frowned. “The what on what roof?”

He tossed her an irritated look. “This project is my chance to prove I know what I’m doing with solar energy. Not so easy when the community center is wedged against that bluff and doesn’t get much sunshine.”

Eden clapped her hand over her mouth. She’d been at the neighborhood meeting that agreed to hire him, but she’d thought he was probably some old guy. What was his name? “Jacob?”

He blinked. “Yes. Have we met?” He looked her up and down, his narrowed gaze lingering on the tattoo on her left arm. “I’m sure I’d remember if we had.”

She lifted her chin. Really? A man in his twenties stuffy

about a tasteful tattoo? He could wipe that sneer off his face. "No, we haven't met. I heard you'd been hired. I didn't know we were neighbors." Just her luck. Cute neighbor, into environmental stuff, but stuck up.

She hoisted Pansy into her arms and eyed the path past him to the door. "I should be going."

"Wait. How did you get back here?" Jacob crossed his arms.

Heat flared up her face. "I came through your house," she mumbled. "Sorry. I heard you yelling at Pansy, and I didn't think. I just ran through."

He shook his head. "Let me escort you back the way you came." He gestured at the open patio door. "After you. And don't let her loose in the house."

As if.

Bang. Thud, thud, bang.

Jacob Riehl glared at the fence just ten feet away. The whole structure seemed to vibrate as Eden attacked it with a hammer. At least, he assumed that's what she was doing.

He could just imagine her crouched in the grass on the other side, biting her lip in concentration as she tried to pound the nails in to secure the loose board. Maybe the goat nibbled at her blond-with-a-tinge-of-strawberry ponytail.

A goat in the city.

He'd heard the bleating a few times in the two weeks since he'd moved in next door with his buddy, Logan. They'd looked up the animal bylaws and found that Spokane did, indeed, allow goats and other livestock in this neighborhood near the downtown core. So long as they were well contained and cared for, of course.

Too bad this rental was close to both his and Logan's jobs, to say nothing of the community center he'd been hired to outfit with solar panels. His gut soured as he stared at the remains of his report, due in just three days. The vertical plank fence had looked solid, but he hadn't walked the length of it and poked every board. Apparently he should have.

Thud. Bang.

Sounded like Eden was missing the nail more often than hitting it. Didn't she know that screws would hold the board tighter?

Thud. Thwack.

"Ow! Ow, ow, ow."

Good to hear his neighbor wasn't one for cursing. Jacob stared at the barricade. Man, he wasn't going to get any peace unless he went over there and fixed it himself.

"Pan-zeeee!" yelled Eden.

That did it. Jacob surged to his feet, scooped the papers off the patio table — who knew if that goat was going to escape again? — and strode into the house. His drill was in the hall closet, right where it belonged. A quick trigger-pull proved it had plenty of juice. He selected a bag of screws from the stacked bins then marched out the front door, around to the side gate next door, and right in without so much as a knock.

The goat bleated and side-hopped toward him.

Eden whirled and dropped her hammer. "Ouch!" she yelped, rubbing her foot. "You scared me."

"Sorry I didn't knock." Jacob reached behind him for the gate latch. Maybe he shouldn't assume she wanted help. But, no. He was doing it to make sure that menace didn't get back into his space. It wasn't to help Eden so much, and certainly not to get a closer look at her… or her tattoo.

She had dirt on her arms, hair pulling out of its ponytail, and clothes obviously chosen for yard work not glamour. Somehow she managed to be pretty despite the mess, her eyes wild as she retrieved the hammer and stood facing him.

Jacob held up the drill. "I thought maybe you could use a hand."

Her gaze flicked to the fence then back at him as a pinkish tinge crept up her face. "I can manage."

"It's no trouble." Actually, it was, but that was beside the point. He wasn't going to get anything done while listening to her pound the board rather than the nail or worse, smash her thumb again. "Please. Let me help." He took a few steps closer, trying to keep his eyes on her face, but… roses? Why would she have roses tattooed around her bicep?

Eden crossed her arms and widened her stance.

Guess he hadn't done a good enough job of blanking his expression. "I only want to be neighborly. It sounds like you could use a hand. I have the tools and the ability to use them." Unlike her.

She sighed. "I guess I should be thankful. I prayed for help, so I shouldn't be too picky whom God sends my way."

"Am I that bad?" Jacob narrowed his eyes. "You don't even know me." Then the rest of her words caught up to him. "Did you say you prayed?"

She lifted her chin slightly. "I did. I pray about nearly everything, but it seems God sometimes has a sense of humor in how He answers."

"What do you mean by that?" He might not like the reply, but he had to know.

"I pray about everything because God hears and cares about me and my troubles."

Jacob waved a hand. "No, I meant about the humor."

"Huh?"

"You said—"

"I know what I said. Are you telling me you're not making fun of the fact that I pray?"

"Why would I? I pray all the time myself, only I never really thought about God laughing at me when He answers." He'd also never thought about a tattooed woman praying.

"Not laughing, exactly." The goat leaned against Eden's leg, and she crouched down to rub the scruffy head. "I was so embarrassed about Pansy getting in your yard and eating your papers. Why couldn't God have sent an answer that didn't make me feel even more stupid and inept?"

Was there supposed to be a valid reply to that? "I'm pretty sure God sent me." It suddenly seemed clear, anyway. "You wouldn't want to tell God you didn't like His answer, would you?"

"I didn't say..." Her words faded away, and her face took on a brighter hue. "Never mind."

Interesting. But he didn't have all day. "Let me at that fence?"

She nodded and backed up a few steps.

A quick glance at the boards in the vicinity of the loose one indicated that any of them might work its way free next. He might as well plan on doing the whole side, just to keep his yard secure.

The goat butted Jacob's leg, and he winced. That could leave a bruise. Why would anyone want to own a goat, anyway?

"How can I help?"

"Keep her out of my way." He spied an enclosure farther back. "Like in there." A ramp led up to the fenced rooftop of a small lean-to. It must be the goat's domain, even though several hens scratched in the dirt around the base. Man, she had a veritable farm.

"I don't think so." Eden's fists found her hips. "She spends enough time locked up when I'm at work."

Jacob frowned, pointing his drill at the fence. "Isn't that what led to the problem in the first place? She's an animal. Put her in the pen."

"No." Eden leaned a little closer, blue eyes sparking. "She's my family. She'll be fine in the yard."

He could think of all kinds of things to say about someone who looked at a goat as a family member. Her eyes dared him to say them.

Just then, Pansy picked up a metal bucket and tossed it over her shoulder, missing his leg by mere inches. The goat lowered her head and stared at him.

Seemed both females in the space trusted him equally. Excellent start, Riehl. Excellent start.

Chapter 2

"HEY! BRING THAT back here."

Oh, no. Eden had only turned away from the goat for a few seconds to refill the chickens' water. She pivoted, hose in hand, and directed a stream of water at Pansy with her thumb.

Pansy thought it was a game, just like everything else. This time she had Jacob's bag of screws in her mouth. Thankfully it was plastic, not paper.

Eden directed the spray more forcefully as she edged closer to Pansy. Goats might have a cast-iron stomach, but that didn't make two-inch brass screws edible. In her periphery, Jacob approached Pansy from a different angle. Maybe between them, they could corner her and get the bag away. Or at least back her into the pen... Yes, that might work, for all that Eden had advocated the goat's freedom. There'd be a smaller area to work in.

Eden snapped the gate shut behind Pansy, leaving Jacob on the other side, as the goat bounded up the makeshift ramp to the roof. Of course.

"Why do you have a pen for her if you don't keep her in it?"

"I told you. It's for when I'm at work." Eden didn't bother to glance at him. Pansy required every speck of her attention. He'd never understand, anyway.

"Women."

The half-mutter did it. She pivoted at the top of the ramp, blocking Pansy onto the small fenced rooftop. "She gets lonely. Did you keep your dog in its kennel even when you were home?"

"My dog?"

"That's what I said."

"I never had a dog."

"You nev... what?" She could almost feel sorry for the guy. Almost. "Where did you grow up, anyway?"

His blue eyes narrowed. "Portland. My parents didn't allow pets. Other than goldfish."

"Fish aren't pets."

"I could say the same about goats."

"And you'd be wrong," she shot back. "Pansy is sweet and loves to cuddle. If you've ever tried to snuggle a goldfish, you might get the difference."

"My fish never escaped like this Houdini. They never stole my screws. Fish are very soothing to watch." Jacob shrugged. "I'll take fish any day."

And to think she'd admired his muscles. How much less manly could he be than to prefer goldfish over dogs? She could understand his antipathy toward goats, at least at the moment. But if he remained her neighbor, he'd soon understand. How could anyone be around Pansy for long and not fall in love?

"Maa!"

Eden whirled and grabbed the bag of screws from the

deck. "Thank you." She crouched and scratched the goat's head.

Pansy leaned hard against her and nestled in. About the only thing wrong with goats was that they didn't purr. Licorice would totally be rumbling by this stage. Not that the black tom would have gotten into so much trouble to begin with.

"Toss me the bag?"

Oh, yeah. Jacob.

Eden's face burned as she gave Pansy one final pat and hurried down the ramp. Maybe it would be best to leave her in the pen, after all, while Jacob worked, even though it went against every grain in Eden's body. She clicked the gate shut behind her and handed the bag to her neighbor. "Sorry about that." She snuck a glance up at his firm jaw and short, curly hair.

His blue eyes blazed back at her.

What was he thinking?

He shook his head slightly and turned to the fence. "Your yard would be in better shape if you kept her in the pen."

Eden stiffened. "She saves on mowing." But he had a point. The space was rather ugly, when she tried to see it through someone else's eyes. More like a corral than a backyard. "Besides, I have flowers and herbs out front."

The buzz of the drill grinding in a screw drowned her words.

Right. He had a job to do. A job she should have done herself. Maybe she should buy herself one of those drills. No doubt screws would hold up better than nails, not taking into account that she couldn't swing even her lightweight hammer to save her life.

Jacob set down the drill and grabbed her hammer off the ground then used it to give two sharp taps to one of the nails. He shook his head. "I'll be right back."

Where was he going? What was he doing?

He disappeared out the side gate and reappeared a few minutes later with a full-size hammer. He held it up for her inspection. "If you're going to do real work, you need real tools."

Eden bit her lip. Was it so wrong to be a girly-girl and have smaller, pink tools? She didn't have his muscles, which flexed as he gave a single solid whack to the errant nail. He moved down the fence, setting various protruding nail heads into the vertical boards.

She should stop staring. He wasn't doing it because he liked her. On the contrary, he did it to safeguard his own property next door.

He walked back to where he'd left the drill. "I'm surprised your landlord lets you get away with this."

"I own this house." Free and clear, thanks to her parents' estate, not that he needed to know.

"That explains a lot."

"Wait just a minute, buster. I didn't ask you to come here and insult me."

He hefted the drill and met her gaze. She parked both hands on her hips and shot as many daggers at him as she could muster. After a long moment, he looked away.

"I know you're just doing it to keep Pansy from coming in your yard and destroying something else. I totally get that. Don't think I'm not sorry for what she did or grateful for your help. But I could do without the rude comments."

"You're right. I'm sorry." He let out a long breath and a lopsided smile curved his mouth. "My condemning fault is wanting everything in its place. My sister tells me life isn't as black and white as I'd like." He glanced up at Pansy, still watching them from the roof of her shed. "Even her."

Wait. Had he made a joke? Because Pansy was mostly black, with just a touch of white. "She has a bit of gray," Eden offered. "By one hoof and behind her ears."

He was actually kind of good-looking when he grinned. "So she does." He turned back to Eden. "Look, I am sorry. Not only was I not acting very neighborly, I know God isn't pleased by my attitude. I just..." He hesitated then shrugged. "It doesn't matter what my excuses were." He held out his hand. "Truce?"

She reached out and gave his hand a firm shake. "Here's to new beginnings." His hand was warm and more callused than she'd have guessed just looking at him, although those biceps hadn't materialized from thin air. He might not have any animals, but apparently that didn't keep him from getting exercise.

Cute and muscular only went so far. Anyone who loved her would have to love Pansy, Licorice, the chickens, and any other animals that came along. Her face flushed as she pulled her hand away. Now that had been a random thought. She wasn't looking for love.

"So you got roped into fixing the neighbor's fence?" Logan leaned against the counter, a tall glass of pop, clinking with ice cubes, in his hand.

"Did you see what that stupid goat did to my presentation?" Jacob growled.

His roommate grinned. “Thankfully, the slobber has dried.”

“You’re such a comfort.”

“I try. So tell me about our neighbor.”

Jacob shook his head. “A gi... woman. she’s about our age, I’d guess.”

Logan’s eyebrows rose. “With a goat?”

“Apparently you don’t have to be a certain age to get a permit for animals.”

“Glad the Riehl humor is intact.”

Oh, man. He was doing it again, wasn’t he? He’d found a sense of satisfaction with every screw he’d set in place, but his improved mood had evaporated when he returned home and saw the stack of goat-worn papers on the counter.

“I’m ordering in pizza.” His night to cook, but he was abdicating. “I have a lot of work to redo before Tuesday’s meeting.”

“Your cash, your call.” Logan leveraged away from the counter and drained his glass in one long swallow. “Skip the anchovies, if you don’t mind.” He set the glass onto the counter and wandered into the living room.

Jacob shook his head, rinsed the glass, and put it in the dishwasher. He placed the order then followed Logan into the other room and yanked the jack out of the electronic keyboard.

Logan looked up at him as the crescendo of the worship song he’d been playing surged into the house. “Didn’t know you wanted to listen,” he said a moment later, draping his headphones around his neck.

Jacob dropped onto the nearest armchair. “I could use a dose of center.”

His roommate’s fingers drifted over the keyboard as he

watched Jacob. "Tell me about our neighbor."

"She has a tattoo."

Logan chuckled. "Sounds like you don't approve of her. Is she pretty? Where does she work?"

"It doesn't matter if I approve. She's my neighbor, not my girlfriend." As for pretty… he didn't really want to answer that. "Get this. She works for animal control. Now if that isn't ironic, I don't know what is."

"Cute, huh?"

"Didn't say that."

"You avoided the question." Logan grinned. "Figured if she was homely, you'd have mentioned it."

"Doesn't matter what she looks like."

"But it matters if she has a tat?" Logan's fingers picked out the refrain from one of Jacob's favorite choruses.

Jacob let out a long breath. "Nope, that doesn't matter, either. The only thing that matters is making sure her goat doesn't get in our yard again. I feel kind of violated." Not only the goat, but then having Eden walk through the house and into the backyard without invitation. Who did that, anyway? Someone chasing her goat, apparently.

"Too bad you fixed the fence."

"What are you talking about? You can't possibly want escaped animals in our yard, eating everything in sight."

"You're right. But offering to fix it would have been a great way to meet her. Now I need to think of something else."

Jacob leaned forward, elbows on his knees. "Meet her why?"

"To see why she's got you in such a flap. You might be content in Spokane without a girlfriend, but I'd be downright happy to meet someone." Logan's eyebrows rose and fell in time with the music. “With or without a tattoo.”

“Well, she’s a Christian, so she’s got that going for her.”

The music stopped in mid-measure with near-deafening silence. “Why didn’t you say so?”

“Why would I have? I didn’t know you were going to go all caveman at the thought of a pretty girl next door.”

“Ahhh. So she is pretty. Getting any information out of you is crazy difficult, Riehl. What else can you tell me? Which church does she go to? Might be a place to try this week.”

Jacob shook his head and raised both hands. “How should I know?” The doorbell rang, and he surged to his feet. Awfully quick for pizza delivery, but he’d take it. He was starving.

Chapter 3

THE CLOSING CHORDS OF the final song drifted away. Eden slowly lowered her hands and took a deep breath. If only she could live on the weekly high of an emotional worship service. Her own quiet time at home was precious, but something about the music, the gathering of friends, and the pastor's words made Sunday mornings her favorite time of the week.

An elbow poked her ribs. "Hubba hubba," breathed Hailey.

Could her best friend not wait three seconds before checking out the guys? Not that Eden was completely immune, of course. The little church near the downtown core was growing steadily, thanks to solid teaching from their new pastor, who was forty-something and married with kids, to Hailey's disappointment.

"Two of them." Hailey stared past Eden's shoulder. "We have died and gone to heaven."

Eden shook her head but couldn't keep a small grin from poking at the corners of her mouth. Nor could she resist sending a glance behind her.

Jacob Riehl stood beside a guy with shaggy shoulder-length blond hair and shook hands with Tad Amato, who'd been seated in front of them. Jacob wrinkled his nose and made a face at Tad's toddler, who grinned shyly back.

Huh. He'd spent most of yesterday scowling, not smiling. He turned slightly, catching Eden watching him. He acknowledged her with a little nod, then focused back on Tad and the little one.

"Wait a minute," whispered Hailey. "Who is that? Have you already met and didn't tell me?"

Eden turned her back on the men across the sanctuary. "Oh, the guy with the haircut is my next-door neighbor. Not sure who the other one is."

"Introduce me?" Hailey grabbed Eden by both shoulders and stared deeply into her eyes. "Please? I'll give you a free cinnamon roll every day for a month."

"You're crazy." Just last year Hailey and her cousin had re-opened the bakery their grandparents had left them, and the cinnamon rolls were to die for. The dough was perfect, and the tingle of cinnamon and brown sugar melting on Eden's tongue never lasted long enough. "Thirty cinnamon rolls?"

Hailey held up her hand, palm out. "I solemnly swear."

One moment of embarrassment. Thirty cinnamon rolls.

"I'll even bring them to your house."

Eden rolled her eyes. "The fence is too tall to watch the neighbor from my backyard."

"But I might see him out front. Please?"

"Whatever." She might as well get this over with. "I'll pick up the first one tomorrow morning on my way to work."

Hailey squeezed Eden's hands. "You're the best."

Eden edged out of the row ahead of her friend. The two

men had made their way to the back, where the pastor's wife engaged them in conversation. If they disappeared too quickly, Eden would miss out on a month of treats. She smiled and nodded at various church members as she briskly wended her way toward the foyer, Hailey all but stepping on her heels.

Jacob turned toward her when she was mere feet away. "Hi, Eden. Is this where you usually go to church?"

"It is." She smiled at the pastor's wife. "Good morning, Juanita."

Something pointy jabbed the middle of her back.

"Say, Jacob, I'd like you to meet my friend Hailey North. She and her cousin own the Bridgeview Bakery and Bistro over on West Main. Hailey, this is Jacob Riehl from Portland, my next door neighbor."

"I'm so pleased to meet you." Hailey took Jacob's hand between both of hers, sounding as breathless as if she'd jogged half a mile, something Hailey would never do in a million years. "What brings you to Spokane?"

Jacob glanced from Hailey to Eden and back again. Eden lifted her shoulder in a slight shrug. She'd done her bit. Let the cinnamon start rolling.

"I work for Global Sunbeams." Jacob angled his head toward the other man. "This is Logan Dermott. We met on a missions trip in Africa a couple of years ago, and we're renting a place together for now."

Hailey managed to remove one hand from Jacob's and reach for Logan. "That's wonderful! I'm so happy to meet both of you. How about you, Logan? What do you do for a living?"

"I work in construction."

"Oh, how fascinating."

Eden cringed.

Not that Hailey was done yet. "Hey, Eden and I were heading out for lunch. Would you guys like to join us?"

They were? Since when? Eden died a little death inside. Hailey had better double the cinnamon rolls. There'd been nothing about continued embarrassment in their deal.

"Sure, why not?" Logan rocked on his heels. "Where's good?"

Jacob shot a sharp look at his friend. Interesting.

"Frank's Diner is always great," said Hailey. "And it's not that far from here."

"It's always busy at Sunday lunch. We'll probably have to wait." Eden checked her watch then shrugged. She'd been dragged into this and she'd make the best of it, one way or the other.

Jacob brightened. "I've wanted to try that place. They buy a lot of local ingredients, don't they?"

Eden pulled back and took a closer look at him. "They do." And a guy who appreciated that should be nicer to her goat.

"Well, then, yeah, let's do it." Jacob nodded at Logan, and apparently the matter was settled.

"Do you know how to find it?" asked Hailey. "It's a bit complicated with the one-way streets and the roundabout. I could ride with you and—"

"No, we're good."

Eden hid her grin at Jacob's quick reply.

"It's just south of the fire station, isn't it?" he continued. "I've driven by. We can find it."

Hailey pursed her lips then tossed her short blond hair back. "Okay then. We'll meet you there in a few minutes."

Eden curled her fingers around Hailey's arm and all but

dragged her away when it seemed her friend had more to say. "You owe me big time," she muttered when she hoped they were out of audible range.

Hailey pulled free. "What do you mean? A cinnamon roll a day for a month. That's what we agreed on."

"That was before you made a fool of yourself inviting them for lunch."

"I did not!" Hailey whirled around on the church steps and parked both hands on her hips. "I just didn't want to waste the opportunity."

Eden rolled her eyes. "They think you're a stalker. Seriously, girl. There needs to be more than thirty cinnamon rolls coming my way for that embarrassment. Either double it, or toss in a loaf of bread every week."

Hailey narrowed her gaze. "I wasn't really that bad." A rueful expression crossed her face.

"Yeah, you were."

"I'm sorry. It's just that we so rarely get new blood—"

"Doesn't mean you have to make a fool of yourself."

"Okay, okay." Hailey held up both hands. "Point taken. Should we cancel?"

Now that was a temptation. Even as she thought it, Eden shook her head. "That's even worse. You can redeem yourself by being pleasant and not desperate over lunch, though."

Hailey grimaced. "Fine."

"Don't forget the extra cinnamon rolls." Eden jingled her car keys. "Ready?"

Frank's Diner had been created from an old presidential rail car. When the foursome finally got called for their booth,

Jacob could see why there'd been a wait. The ambience was awesome, but there wasn't much seating.

Ahead of him, Eden edged into one side and Hailey took the bench across from her. Great, now they were going to look like two couples. No doubt what Hailey had in mind. Jacob had never experienced such blatant flirting. Thankfully Logan was ahead of him, leaving Jacob with the last seat. He didn't have to choose, which didn't stop him from being slightly disappointed when Logan slid in beside Eden. Hailey beamed at him. Uh oh.

A waitress slipped a stack of menus to the table and took their drinks order. "What's good here?" He opened a menu.

"Everything." Hailey's elbow brushed his arm.

If he shifted any further over, he'd fall into the aisle, and the waitress would trip over him. Jacob met Eden's eyes across the table. "What do you think?"

She shrugged her shoulder. "Hailey's right. I've never been unhappy with anything I've ordered."

"So what are you having today?"

Eden smacked the menu closed. "The Jalapeno Pepper Jack Bacon Burger."

Jacob glanced at the entry. Too hot? Or not? "I'll give it a try."

"Ditto." Logan gathered the menus and set them on the end of the table. After placing their order, he angled toward Eden. "Have you lived in Spokane long?"

The two women exchanged a glance. "I'm a lifer," said Eden.

"Me, too. Eden and I went to the same school when we were kids."

"Private school?" asked Jacob.

Eden narrowed her gaze at him across the table. "Public."

He kept forgetting not everyone had lived his life. She was probably mortgaged to the hilt to purchase even a rickety old house like hers. Just because she valued home ownership didn't mean she had grown up with money. He carefully did not look at her tattooed roses. How much had those things cost, anyway? He'd never been tempted enough to look into it. Besides, he'd have been expelled from his elite school for getting one. And now? Why bother? He wasn't that fond of pain, and he couldn't think of a statement he wanted to make badly enough to etch it into his skin.

What kind of statement did a bunch of roses make? Jacob blinked the thought away. That wasn't a question he'd ever ask.

Hailey watched him from blue eyes. "Private school, hey? What was that like?"

Jacob shrugged. "My normal. I could ask you the same about public." But he wouldn't. He shouldn't have accepted her invitation to start with, the way she batted her eyelashes at him. It made him uncomfortable. He'd always been the geeky guy, too focused on grades to overcome his awkwardness and date. His sisters had teased him, but he'd seen the string of boyfriends left in the wake of Sierra, the oldest, especially. Growing up, he'd kind of felt sorry for them. Of course she was happily married now with four adopted kids, but Jacob hadn't forgotten.

He wasn't going to start dating until he was ready to get married. He jerked back with a start, and the waitress slipped plates onto the table. What had he been waiting for? He was an adult. Finished school. Had a decent job.

Whoa.

He wouldn't date or marry a woman like Hailey. Anyone that desperate, he had to wonder why. Nor anyone like Eden.

What guy wanted to trace a woman's tattoo with his fingertips? Not him. But someone? Was he really ready to start thinking about settling down?

"And then Jacob flipped the switch. You should have seen their faces light up, just like the room."

He blinked back into reality as Logan nodded at him from across the table. "Remember that, Jacob?"

Switch. Faces. Light. "You mean in Limpopo?" The aroma of the burger and fries in front of him vied with memories of the deep-fried Mopane worms he hadn't been able to bring himself to try in Africa.

Logan angled his head. "Isn't that what I said?"

"Right." Jacob glanced at Eden beside Logan. "That was awesome." Unlike the food there. Focus, Riehl. Pay attention to the conversation.

Hailey leaned against his arm. "I've never been anywhere that interesting. A girlfriend and I spent a summer in Glasgow, but then Scotland is a first-world country."

Jacob shifted away and felt his balance precarious. A glance at Eden and Logan proved the seats were plenty wide enough for two. "Uh, would you mind scooting over a bit? I'm nearly falling off here."

A strangled sound came from Logan, whose lips twitched even as he stared somewhere past Jacob's head.

"Oh, sorry." Hailey's perfume lingered as she shifted a few inches closer to the window. "Is that better?"

Eden dipped her head, raised her eyebrows, and gave her friend the look. Hailey slid over a bit more.

"Yes, thanks." So it hadn't been his imagination. Hailey was coming onto him, and he had no idea how to handle it. He wasn't the slightest bit interested, but she couldn't seem to catch a clue.

Hailey chatted brightly about her summer in Glasgow then shifted seamlessly into her life as a small-business owner. When she stopped for a sip of her drink, Jacob plunged in. “Tell us about a trip you’ve made, Eden.” Anything to stop Hailey.

She paused, burger halfway to her mouth, and angled a look at Hailey before turning her gaze to him. “I haven’t really traveled, but I’d love to hear more about Africa.”

Great. The ball was back in his court. If he only remembered what Logan had said while he’d been tuned out. Wondering if he were ready for marriage. The beginnings of a flush crept up his neck. “Logan’s a better storyteller than I am.” He lifted his burger. “A bit of heat in this, but it’s sure good.”

Chapter 4

HAILEY LEANED BACK IN the passenger seat and closed her eyes, a dreamy smile playing around her lips. “Ah. We have died and gone to heaven.”

Jamming her key into the ignition of her aging car, Eden glared at her friend. “Would you stop saying that?”

“How could you spend over an hour with those two hunks and not be affected?”

“Hunks?” Eden shook her head. “That’s not the word I’d use.”

Hailey straightened and turned toward her. “Then what?”

“They’re just regular guys. Nothing special.” She turned left onto West 2nd. They could practically have walked home more quickly than driving, thanks to the steep hill and all the one-way streets.

“Well, if you’re not in the game, which one should I pick? I think Jacob is cuter, but he seems rather quiet and brooding, don’t you think?”

Did that require a reply?

“But Logan is pretty hot, too. Seems more like a guy who knows how to have fun. He’d have to get a haircut, though.”

"What's wrong with his hair?"

"Don't you think it's a bit long for a man? I'm not sure I like it."

"Hailey. Stop it already. You met the guy two hours ago."

"What's that got to do with anything? Don't you believe in love at first sight?"

"No, I don't. That's ridiculous. Neither of those guys is interested in you."

Hailey crossed her arms over her chest. "Oh, now you're the expert?"

"I've studied body language. Jacob would rather fall off the bench than brush against you accidentally, and the look he gave you was not that of a man in love. He was plain irritated."

"I don't think—"

"And that's exactly the problem. What you're doing is signaling desperation."

"I'm twenty-five, Eden. A quarter of a century old. With no prospects. I am going to die an old maid."

"I'm twenty-five, too."

"I know. You should feel time marching on as much as I do. Our biological clocks are ticking, girl. Don't you want to have babies?"

"Sure, but I'm fine with not starting this week." She parked the car in front of the bakery and turned to her friend. "Hailey, you know I love you. We've been best friends since we were five years old. But… really."

Hailey shoved the car door open. "So what's your problem? I didn't do anything wrong."

Eden managed to hold back the impulse to glance heavenward.

"How is a guy going to know a girl is interested if she

doesn't show it?"

"It might not hurt to leave something for the second meeting."

"Why, Eden Andrusek. If I didn't know better, I'd think you were jealous."

As if. "You're embarrassing."

Hailey swung out of the car. "If I humiliate you so much, you won't want the cinnamon rolls, right? It will be like taking blood money."

The idea that Hailey might take her any more seriously if she gave up her right to them had crossed Eden's mind, but the mere thought of the brown sugar and cinnamon melting on her tongue made her knees go wobbly. She'd won those fair and square. "You're not getting out of it that easily."

Hailey's eyes gleamed as she leaned back into the car. "So it's not that bad then."

"Two separate issues, my friend. I earned those cinnamon rolls. I'll stop by on my way to work in the morning, thanks."

"I'm not giving you free coffee to go with it."

"I'm not too proud to drink office coffee."

Hailey laughed and tucked her hair behind her ear. "You're incorrigible."

"I can keep Pansy in food for the cost of organic drinks from your bakery."

"You and that goat. Her feed cost should come out of the price you get for the cheese and milk. If she's not paying her own way, she's nothing but a pet."

And how was that bad? "How did we get from cinnamon rolls to whether Pansy is a pet or not?"

"Whatever." Hailey shook her head. "I'll see you in the morning." She shut the car door and stood on the sidewalk in front of the renovated bakery, waving as Eden pulled away.

A few blocks west sat the old brick building that was being turned into a community center. Originally a school, it had been an art gallery before the recession of ’08, when even rich people hadn’t been able to justify the price of art anymore. Eden had gone in there plenty of times as a teen, dreaming of the day she could afford an original Robert Bateman or Liz Lesperance painting. She’d imagined it hanging on a two-story gallery wall in her big house in Glenrose.

She pulled into the rutted driveway of her small house in Bridgeview, a far cry from her dreams. Truth? She didn’t really want the mansion anymore. Bridgeview was tight and friendly and safe, if one didn’t count the wildlife along the river. Still, she’d certainly not planned to keep living in the house where she’d grown up.

The fiery crash that took her parents and two sisters had changed everything. The house was her consolation prize. She fingered the tattoo. Every painful moment in the chair had reminded her she was alive when she didn’t deserve to be.

Tears prickled her eyes, and she shoved open the car door. Enough. She’d weed Mom’s rosebushes this afternoon. That would be her penance for forgetting, even a little while.

“Look, we signed a one-year lease.” Logan leveled a glare at Jacob from the driver’s seat. “I don’t have the money to burn to buy our way out of it. Plus, I like this area with the river across the street and all. It’s close enough to down-tow—”

"Yeah, yeah. I remember all the reasons we decided to take this place." Jacob rubbed the spot on his scalp where a headache was trying to get a grip.

"At least it's not Hailey who lives next door." Logan turned at the end of the block.

Now that was a mercy.

A woman knelt in the flowerbed at the house beyond theirs. Jacob narrowed his gaze. Not Eden, too? She'd seemed quiet at lunch. She certainly hadn't displayed the same blatant flirting her friend had. But why else is she out beside the driveway?

"Because she lives there and there are weeds?"

He blinked. "Did I say that out loud?"

Logan let out a guffaw as he turned into their short drive. "You so did."

Jacob would have to get out of the passenger side three feet from Eden. "We need a place with a garage."

"Give it up, dude. Live dangerously. I bet your parents didn't get that four-thousand-square-foot house with its three-car garage straight out of college."

He blew out a long breath. "You're right. I just had no idea how expensive everything would be, or how far my salary wouldn't go. They made it look so easy."

"Your mom's an optometrist with her own clinic. She must bank pretty good coin."

"I guess." He hadn't really thought much about it growing up. Like his friends, he'd never been denied anything he needed. Same could be said for just about everything he'd wanted, from soccer cleats as an eight-year-old to a high-end computer at thirteen to the hybrid BMW for graduation. "Maybe I should reconsider trying to get into the big firm by River Park Square. They were impressed with my resume."

Logan raised his eyebrows. “Tell me again why you turned them down.”

“Because Global Sunbeams funds installations in third world countries.”

“Uh huh. And that matters to you why?”

Jacob glared at his friend. “You know why.”

“Seems like you need reminding.” Logan poked with his chin. “Keep talking. I’m listening.”

“Because going to Africa with my brother-in-law and bringing dependable light and an energy source to entire villages changed my life.”

“Did it?”

Jacob stared at his friend. “What do you mean?”

“Sounds like you’re still pining for the lifestyle of the rich and famous.”

He sighed. “I hear you, man. It’s hard giving it all up. When I was in Limpopo with Keanan, helping the poor seemed like the coolest thing in the world. I’m just not really fond of being poor myself.”

Logan grinned. “The folks at the homeless shelter might figure you are still pretty rich. It’s all perspective.”

“You’re right. I know it.” Jacob leveled a glare. “Don’t let it go to your head.”

“Never, dude. I’m sure she’s wondering by now why we’re still sitting in the car.”

Right. Eden.

Jacob pushed the door open, and she settled back on her heels as she looked up. She wiped the back of a gloved hand over her forehead. “Hi.”

She’d changed out of the pink floral sleeveless dress with the heels and the chunky pink necklace she’d worn to church and lunch. She was back to jeans cut into shorts at mid-thigh and a light green tank top. Uh, not that he was paying attention. No matter what she wore, those roses danced in front of his eyes.

He jerked his gaze back to her face.

"Maa."

The goat. Where was she?

Pansy trotted out from the shadows beside the house.

Just... loose?

Eden reached over and rubbed Pansy's head around her halter. "Did you have a good nap?" she crooned.

Jacob peered closer. That was a tether dragging behind the animal, wasn't it?

Eden sighed. "She's tied, Jacob. She's not going to run off and get in trouble."

He still had a lot of that paperwork to redo. "That's good. I'd hate to call animal control."

She glared at him.

"So this is the infamous goat." Logan came around the front of the car. "Hey, she's kind of cute. What breed is she?"

Eden's eyes brightened. "A Nigerian dwarf. City bylaws allow goats and sheep that stand up to twenty-four inches at the shoulder." Pansy plopped down, head in Eden's lap.

Jacob rubbed his forehead again. Why was he so bothered by Eden Andrusek and her goat? Yeah, the papers. That had been a bad start, but it was something more. More than the tattoo. It was—

"Pansy!" called a young voice.

A girl, towed by a large dog, ran ahead of her mother and brother toward Eden. That dog could eat the goat in three bites. Okay, maybe four. Eden should be panicking, but instead she grinned at the child.

The dog woofed a greeting then crouched, wagging its

tail. The little goat leaped onto the dog's back, but the girl grabbed Pansy around the neck and hugged her so hard the goat toppled against her.

"Violet, take it easy." Her mom was halfway up the driveway by now, a pretty woman with brown hair brushed back into a long ponytail.

"I love Pansy." The girl squished the goat. "She makes the best cheese ever."

She what? Jacob pulled back.

"Technically, it's Eden who makes the cheese." The woman laughed, then seemed to notice the guys for the first time. "Hi, you must be our new neighbors. I'm Adriana Diaz, and these are my kids, Sam and Violet."

"Logan Dermott. And my housemate, Jacob Riehl. We moved in a couple of weeks ago."

"Oh, Marietta told me all about you both. Welcome to Spokane." Adriana pointed upward at the bridge. "And to Bridgeview. We live around the end of the block."

Bridgeview. When Logan had told him about the rental, Jacob had assumed they'd have a great view of a bridge. He hadn't expected it to be the underside of one. This neighborhood was nestled deep in the valley downriver from the falls, with the bridge itself soaring above the Spokane River as well as the streets and homes below.

Jacob pushed aside his annoyance at the overhead bridge. It wasn't Adriana's fault. Nor Eden's, for that matter. "Pleased to meet you."

Violet bounced in front of Eden. "Can I feed her a carrot? Can I?"

"May I," Adriana corrected.

"Sure."

"C'mere, Pansy. I have a snack for you."

"We came to pick up our milk." Adriana glanced toward Jacob then refocused on Eden. "If it's not a bad time."

"No, it's perfect." Eden got to her feet and dusted the garden dirt from her shorts. "Did you need any cheese?"

"Not today. May I put in an order for next week?"

"Sure. No problem." Eden turned to the boy. "Want to come with me, Sam? I see you have your backpack."

The boy wore glasses and looked to be about seven or eight. He nodded, adjusting the straps of his pack, and fell into step beside Eden as they headed for the side gate. He seemed a lot quieter than his younger sister, who chatted at Pansy as though the goat were deaf.

"Have you lived in Spokane long?" asked Logan.

"I came here for college, fell in love, and stayed."

Spokane wasn't bad, but Jacob couldn't envision falling in love with it, precisely. He was here because it was close enough to connect with his sisters and their families in Galena Landing, Idaho, but urban enough to suit him. Besides, Global Sunbeams was a great mix of business and charity.

"I thought about moving away after Stephan died but, by then, the kids and I had a network here. Friends. The church."

Oh. Heat crept up Jacob's neck. She meant she'd fallen in love with a man.

"I'm sorry to hear of your husband's passing." Good thing Logan was able to string words together.

"Papa died in a fire," announced Violet. "He saved an old lady. He was a hero."

"It must have been a difficult time," Jacob murmured.

"It was. It took a while to face the future, but I had Sam and Violet to think about. They were so young and didn't understand. I had to keep going for them."

What did a guy say to that? Thankfully, Eden and Sam came through the side gate right then. The boy said something and peered up at Eden. She laid her arm across his shoulder and gave him a little hug, smiling back.

Jacob blinked. She was pretty. Not in a movie star way, but more wholesome.

"Violet Diaz! No one gave you permission to undo Pansy's tether."

"Aw, Mom. She doesn't want to be tied up. I'm right here. I won't let her run away."

"Violet."

"Fine. I'm the only one who cares about you, Pansy." Violet caressed the goat's head but seemed to do as she'd been told.

Jacob liked kids but, wow, she was a handful.

Eden stopped beside Violet. "You know she can only be loose in the backyard."

"It's not fair."

"Lots of things in life aren't fair, sweetie. Trust me. But you can't decide for anyone else. Okay?"

Violet crossed both arms in front of her. "Can we go home now, Mom?"

"Sure. Sam has the milk. You take Duke's leash, please." Adriana turned to the guys. "Nice to meet you. I'm sure we'll see you around." The little family headed down the sidewalk the way they had come.

When Jacob glanced back at Eden, he noticed her touching her tattoo with a far away look on her face. What did those roses mean to her, anyway?

Chapter 5

EDEN GLANCED AROUND THE inside of the community center. The construction crew had gutted the building, revealing scuffed red bricks that offered a vibe suiting the neighborhood. She slid into a metal folding chair beside Hailey.

"Hey, Eden!" Kass, the bakery's co-owner, leaned past her cousin.

"Hey, yourself. Where have you been hiding?"

Kass gathered her long red hair and tossed it over her shoulder. "I spent a few days visiting my parents in Galena Landing. I hadn't seen them for more than five minutes at a time since Christmas."

"How are they? What about everyone at Green Acres Farm?"

"My folks are doing well. I stopped out there for dinner one evening. They have a full load of students right now, learning all about market gardening. You took a course there, didn't you?"

Eden nodded. "The animal husbandry one two years ago. I still had to take the certification at Washington State before the city would let me keep Pansy and the chickens, even though I learned tons more at Green Acres."

"Of course." Kass offered a sympathetic smile. "Rules are rules."

"And my job involves knowing them all and making sure people follow them." Eden grimaced. "It sounded more fun once upon a time."

"I bet."

Hailey leaned back against her cousin. "We, on the other hand, are living our dream. Right, Kass?"

Kass shrugged. "Kind of. I sometimes wish I was making more of a difference in people's lives. You know?"

Eden licked her lips. "Your cinnamon rolls are a public service. Trust me."

Hailey smacked at Eden's arm.

"Yes, I heard my cousin bribes people with them."

"It was not a bribe." Hailey swiveled to face Kass, eyes wide.

Eden chuckled. "It was totally a bribe. For a few hours, I regretted accepting it, but since I have twenty-eight more rolls to look forward to, I can live with my conscience."

Would she feel differently if Jacob Riehl seemed interested in Hailey? Maybe. The guy shouldn't get under her skin the way he did. He might be cute, but he was way uptight. Him and his private school. Honestly.

Hailey smirked. "You're not the only one who likes them. We have several customers with standing orders."

"I'm not surprised. They are to die for." Hmm. "You might need to add my name to that list after the month is up. Monday to Friday, anyway."

"You don't need treats on Saturdays?"

"Not enough to come by the bakery on my days off, no. I

have too much to do at home." Like relaxing, if she ever found time around caring for Pansy and the chickens.

"You and your little urban farm." Hailey shook her head.

"I notice you're happy enough to buy eggs from me." Not that five hens could supply more than a fraction of what a bakery required.

"It would sure be easier to buy eggs by the case from a wholesaler than from a dozen backyard flocks."

Kass elbowed her cousin. "But we're committed to sourcing locally where we can and being good neighbors."

"The hens and I thank you." Eden turned as the scraping of metal chairs on the old wood floors caught her attention. There must be forty or fifty people gathered as the room filled up. At the front, Ray Santoro conferred with Jacob beside the podium.

The man wouldn't stay. His type would buy a condo somewhere hip, like Kendall Yards across the river.

Ray braced both hands on the podium. "Buonasera! Good evening, neighbors and friends."

A dozen people hollered a greeting back, including Hailey.

"I'm Raimondo Santoro, your host this evening. We are gathered to finalize the next phase of converting this building into a bona fide community center. Several of you have approached the board of directors with innovative ideas on usage, and we'll go over those quickly before turning the remainder of the meeting over to Jacob Riehl, who will update us on the solar power conversion. Francesca and Jasmine are handing out agendas."

Eden glanced up and accepted a few sets of paper from Jasmine then handed all but one to Hailey. They really ought to start emailing these out in advance to save paper. She'd have to remind Ray.

Her gaze slid down the page but was suddenly snagged by the name Kassidy North. Wait, what? Kass had submitted a suggestion? What on earth was a batch cooking workshop? Eyebrows raised, she shot a glance at her friend, pointing at the paper.

Kass grinned and gave her a thumbs-up.

Huh. Eden leaned back in her chair. Guess she'd learn all about it with everyone else.

"Now, if everyone has an agenda," Ray went on, "we'll get started. First up, Wade Roper with an update on the permaculture project."

The biologist and his wife had moved to the Bridgeview neighborhood the year before. He jogged to the podium, waving a large brown envelope. "We got the grant!"

Cheers, whistles, and stomping greeted his words.

"While the food forest initiative is under the guidance of the Bridgeview community, I'd like to get a few volunteers to help plan the details now that we can move forward. We'll also need volunteers to do the actual labor, most of which will be in the fall and next spring. So if you are interested in helping in either way, let Rebekah or me know."

In the front row, Jasmine Santoro jumped to her feet, waving a hand.

Wade chuckled. "Already have your name down, Jasmine. Anyone else?"

A few others called out, and Wade made notes.

Eden bit her lip. Did she have time to join another committee? She could likely participate in the planting days, anyway. She'd talk to Wade afterward. The biologist was already heading to the seat beside his roundly pregnant wife. Rebekah sure wouldn't be digging in the dirt this summer.

"Next up, batch cooking with Kassidy North, co-owner of Bridgeview Bakery and Bistro. Want to come up, Kass?"

Kass edged past Hailey and Eden then strode to the front. She turned to face the group. "I know we have a lot of very busy people in our neighborhood, and that sometimes makes it difficult to find the time and energy to cook nutritious dinners from scratch. I asked Ray what he thought about using the commercial kitchen we're putting into this building as a place where we could gather in groups and prep out a month's worth of meals at a time. I don't know if anyone here has ever done that sort of thing before, but I've found it to be a lifesaver for me in the past. I simply need to shop for perishables weekly and take a meal starter out of the freezer every morning, so it takes only minutes to put dinner together after work."

"Great idea!" called Adriana.

Eden tried to imagine her life that organized... and failed. But it sure would be nice to have food ready to go when she got home. Sometimes by the time she'd milked Pansy and fed her and the chickens, the thought of a fast-food burger seemed compelling. "I'm in!" she called. At least so long as she had a say in what the meals were.

Ray stepped back to the podium. "You all know where to find Kass at the bakery, so if you have any questions, contact her. Our kitchen is several months away from usable, so we can vote on this program concept at our next meeting. From what Kass said to me, participants would pay for the ingredients at bulk pricing, plus just enough to cover her time and the power usage."

He turned to Jacob. "And that brings us to the main presentation tonight. Jacob?"

Kass edged past Eden, blocking her view for a few seconds. And then there he was. Why did he affect her this way? She didn't even like him. He was too serious. Too snooty. She wasn't the kind of girl that flipped over a guy just because he was cute. And besides, she wasn't looking.

Jacob gripped the podium and gazed out at the gathering. Several dozen people stared back. Some oldsters, like Marietta, some middle-aged, some young folks, and a few little kids.

His neighbors, should he decide to stay in Bridgeview. And why not? Where would he find a community more focused on sustainability? He grinned. His sisters had gotten to him. Not enough to turn him into a ruralist, though.

People smiled back. Huh. That was easy.

"I'm Jacob Riehl, and I'm an architectural engineer. I've been interested in renewable resources since I was a teenager. My older sisters are part of a sustainable community farm in Idaho and, after seeing them in action, I decided to focus on solar energy."

What were Eden and her friends whispering about? He looked over to the other side of the room.

"The industry has taken many giant strides forward in the last decade, becoming more accessible to the average homeowner. Not only that, but solar is a godsend to developing countries where the infeasibility of mass-produced power such as hydro-electric dams, thermal generating stations, or nuclear plants literally keeps millions of people in the dark. I've been privileged to have participated in several trips to rural Africa with Global Sunbeams. Teams set up solar panels and batteries in villages, providing energy to schools, churches, and community centers not unlike this one. In many cases, solar also powers the pump for the water system."

That should prove to Eden he wasn't just a spoiled rich kid. Not that it mattered what she thought.

"The teams also provide solar cookers for each family in the village, and we teach them how to use them. The difference this makes in many women's lives is unfathomable to most Americans. No longer do these women need to dry animal dung or seek out decreasingly available wood for their cook fires. Nor do they need to crouch amid heavy smoke to cook their family's food. This frees up innumerable hours in which they can attend literacy classes or start small businesses. Solar cooking is changing the face of Africa as surely as solar power is."

Applause broke out. Eden clapped lightly, too, but she looked more thoughtful than impressed. Whatever.

"That brings me to Spokane, where I now work with Global Sunbeams fulltime. This is also why I am qualified to help Bridgeview convert this community center to solar energy."

Yeah, he was in the right place, at least for the next year or two. Not that he wanted to live in a rental forever, but Marietta Santoro was as good a landlady as any, keeping an eye out on the whole neighborhood as though she was everyone's grandmother. Looking at the crowd, Jacob realized it was nearly true.

He lifted the sheaf of papers that held his in-depth report. "I have all the specs here for anyone who wants to go through them in greater detail. But for the sake of the general meeting, we have a plan to mount the solar panels on specially-designed towers on the roof, high enough to catch the rays above the bluff and the neighboring buildings. Unlike the usual mounting system, this plan leaves the roof free for other usage." Jacob shrugged. "Like a rooftop garden or beehives or a few solar cookers. Whatever you want."

A buzz began in the group, and Jacob looked at Ray helplessly.

Ray jerked his chin, indicating Jacob should keep going. "That can be decided later. I just wanted you to know the roof will still be accessible."

Voices quieted as folks turned forward again. This time even Eden looked at him with grudging approval. Not that it mattered.

"The final piece to the solar puzzle comes in the form of the revolutionary Tesla Powerwall, so we don't need a room full of lead-acid batteries to store the power. The Tesla unit is wall-mounted, so it takes up no square footage and is pretty enough to go anywhere." He walked over and tapped the bricks near the roughed-in kitchen partition. "This would be a good spot, for example."

Ray came up beside him. "We already have grant approval for this entire installation. Are we ready to let Jacob order the materials and begin construction?" He turned to Jacob. "What does the timeline look like?"

"We have everything in stock at Global Sunbeams except the custom towers. We'll need to hire a welder for that. Then it will be a matter of volunteer hours to assemble the system. So, a month. Maybe a bit more."

Ray turned to the group. "Last chance to block this. Unless anyone can provide a compelling reason right here, right now, to halt this project, I authorize Jacob Riehl and

Global Sunbeams to proceed with this installation. Anyone?"

Jacob met Eden's gaze for a long moment as the others in the space faded out. Her smile quirked to one side, and his stomach did a funny little lurch.

No way. He had nothing in common with Eden Andrusek. He barely even tolerated her. Yeah, he could try to keep telling himself that, but his heart seemed to have decided otherwise.

"Go ahead, then, Jacob. We're ready to get the ball rolling." Ray began the applause, and every man, woman, and child in the community center took to their feet, clapping with him.

Even Eden.

Chapter 6

EDEN DRAGGED HERSELF TO her bike after work on Wednesday. After spending all day tracking down complaints of feral dogs along Latah Creek, all she wanted was to cycle home, put her feet on the ottoman, and stick her nose in a book.

But, no. She'd put off picking up groceries at Main Market Co-op in favor of checking in at the night market across the river in Kendall Yards.

She rode her bike across the Lincoln Street Bridge then turned onto Summit Parkway. A few minutes later she chained her bike to a rail and patted the saddlebags. Soon they'd be full.

The market was in full swing. A woman with a guitar crooned out a country love song, just audible above the voices of the milling crowd. Aromas from the taco truck caused her stomach to grumble. Shopping first, though.

She reached for a basket of strawberries, so red and ripe their sweet fragrance rose to her nostrils, but someone else picked up the basket before she could. She glanced at the white rolled shirtsleeve then up the arm.

Jacob Riehl.

"Sorry. Here, take this one. I'll get another." He held it out to her.

"No, that's okay. There are more." She offered payment to the vendor then tucked a basket inside her bag.

"Do you come here often?" His sleeve brushed against her arm as she strolled toward the next booth.

Eden shifted away from the tantalizing contact. Now he wanted to make small talk? "Most Wednesdays during the season, yes. It's well worth it for those who value fresh local food."

"Good to know. It looks like you can get just about everything here."

She narrowed her gaze at the booth in front of her. He was a conundrum. But wait. What had he said at the meeting last night? She glanced up to find his blue eyes regarding her, not with suspicion, but with some sort of interest. Interest?

Eden struggled for words. "You said something about a sustainable community in Idaho at the meeting. Whereabouts?"

"Oh, my sisters? They both live at a place called Green Acres Farm near Galena Landing. Not many people have heard of it."

Green Acres? Seriously? Eden snapped her mouth shut and blinked. "I've been there. Who are your sisters?" The faces of the various farm residents slid through her mind.

"Really? Sierra Rubachuk and Chelsea Welsh."

"No way!" Though a closer examination revealed that Jacob's blond curly hair was sort of like Chelsea's but much shorter. Faces, though? The women were pretty. The same couldn't be said of Jacob. Thankfully.

"What brought you to Green Acres? It's so far off the

beaten track."

"I took one of their courses a couple of years ago. Animal husbandry with Keanan Welsh and Allison Callahan. Liz Nemesek — Waterman, now — did some of the teaching as well."

"Wow, I never thought I'd meet anyone who'd heard of the place. I mean, outside the immediate area."

"It's not that far from Spokane. Some of the people taking the course with me that winter were from much farther away. There was a couple there from New Hampshire, and someone from Tennessee."

Jacob gave his head a quick shake. "I had no idea."

She tilted her head up at him. "Don't you ever go visit?"

"Well, yeah. I was there a few weeks ago, when we were in the process of moving."

"So surely you must have noticed the big timber frame building beside the driveway." To say nothing of several dozen people working in the market garden this time of year.

He stood facing her in the middle of Summit Parkway, all pretense of shopping gone. "Of course I've seen it. It's been there several years. It's Allison's thing." He shrugged. "She had money to burn from her parents' estate."

Eden's parents had left her a little. Certainly not enough to build and equip a school. Her fingers slid to touch the tattoo. Jacob's gaze followed her movement, and his eyes narrowed. Right. He wasn't really alternative or fringe. He was a city boy who happened to like solar energy. Although he was at the farmers' market.

"The farm school there is a happening place," she managed to get out, dropping her hand. "It's very popular with the foodie folks in Spokane, especially when there's a one-day intensive on a Saturday. Nearly anyone can fit that into their schedule."

"Huh." Jacob shook his head then gestured toward a vegetable vendor nearby. "Is this the best place to buy fresh peas?"

"They're pretty good here."

Jacob's hand pressed lightly against the small of her back as she moved toward the blue tent. The warmth lingered even when the contact was broken. No way. How could she be this hyper-aware of the guy? He barely approved of her, even on the most basic level. The touch meant nothing, just a gentlemanly gesture.

He leaned past her to examine the early peas, greens, and garlic scapes. His shirt collar brushed her shoulder.

Eden took half a step forward, as far as she could go without knocking into the table, but he closed the gap then asked the vendor a question that blurred in Eden's mind. What was going on? She looked up at him to find his face only inches from hers.

"I'll take a pound," Jacob said then seemed to notice her watching him. His blue eyes flared slightly as he met her gaze.

For half an eternity, Eden couldn't look away. The light fragrance of his aftershave caught her senses. The noisy chatter of the market faded. Nothing existed but Jacob Riehl and the light pressure of his chest against her shoulder. Oh, and the hand that had returned to her lower back.

She sucked in a deep breath and blinked, pulling her gaze away as the vendor handed a package of peas to Jacob. Somehow she forced her focus to the man behind the table. "I'll have the same."

He turned from one to the other. "You wanted two pounds?"

"No. I want one."

"But..." He looked between them.

Understanding dawned. "We're not together. We each want a pound of peas."

A grin played with the man's lips, and his eyes twinkled. "Got it. Here you go, ma'am."

Eden fumbled in her purse for payment only to find Jacob had already offered the man her sum. "Thanks," she managed before bolting from the booth.

Jacob faced her again in the middle of the cordoned-off street. "Sorry. I shouldn't have done that."

"You're right. That man thought we were... we were..."

"Married?" Jacob asked, a grin quirking one side of his face.

"A couple, anyway." And while he was a Christian and into sustainability and cute — okay, hot — there was no way this was a guy she could date, let alone marry.

Whoa. Her brain was jumping way ahead. Not ahead. It leaped down a side street where she had no intention of following.

Eden took a deep breath. "Well, it was nice running into you. I need to finish my shopping and get home."

"I was hoping you'd show me the best booths to buy from. I'm a newbie here." He'd wiped the grin from his face, but the glimmer in his eyes lingered.

She shouldn't do this. "I need a jar of honey, so I'm headed over there." She pointed a few booths down. Wait, what was she saying? Had her brain not sent a memo?

"Honey. Sounds good, although I got a bucket from Green Acres. From Sierra. She keeps some hives."

"You should always get honey from as close to home as possible. Jasmine is planning to start two hives over at

Marietta's, and I hope to get on her list when she starts selling it."

Jacob gestured at the booth. "This isn't local enough for you?"

"This apiary is in Spokane Valley, so it's not bad. But Jasmine's bees will gather nectar and pollen from our own neighborhood and ecosystem, so ingesting it will build antibodies to ward off allergies."

That half-grin returned. "You sound just like my sister."

Eden examined his face. "I'm not sure whether that is a compliment or not."

He tossed his head back and laughed. "I'm not sure, either."

Jacob wouldn't have guessed a farmers' market could be this entertaining. He'd expected to dive in, nab some fresh fruit and vegetables, and be back across the river in under half an hour.

But the blocked-off street had some sort of vibe happening. A bluegrass band had taken the stage. Neighbors and friends chatted everywhere: in the middle of the street, blocking entrance to booths, and seated at portable tables near one of several mobile food trucks. Assorted aromas assaulted him, all welcoming. Sizzling sausages, herbs — he couldn't even pick out most of them individually.

Except the floral essence that was all Eden. He followed her from booth to booth, trying to stay near in the surge of the crowd. Following her scent like a hound dog. He paused in his steps for an instant. Whoa. Really?

But she was most attractive. He'd seen her at her worst, wearing grubby work clothes with smudges on her face. He'd seen her in a pretty dress on Sunday. And now in a collared sleeveless blouse, which showed off that tattoo as surely as her khaki shorts outlined a trim backside.

He needed to get a grip. On the other hand, hadn't he recently reminded himself he was twenty-six and ready to settle down? What would his family think of Eden? His sisters would likely approve. Eden was one of their kind. And if his parents approved of Chelsea's hippie husband, Keanan, they could hardly balk at a woman with a tattoo and a goat.

A tattoo and a goat. Yeah, more likely his personal hang-up than his family's.

Eden glanced at him from several feet away. "Coming? I still need to pick up a few packages of meat." She indicated a booth advertising beef, lamb, pork, and chicken.

Jacob closed the gap. "Sure. Maybe I'll get some, too."

Her strawberry-blond hair brushed his cheek as he leaned past her to talk to the seller. Soft, whispery. He couldn't help himself. His hand found its way to the small of Eden's back again. He felt her body tense, but she didn't turn toward him. Probably a good thing, or he'd lose his train of thought completely. As it was, he found it painful to pull away long enough to dig out his wallet and offer his credit card to the vendor. He'd spent all his cash already.

Eden faced him in the street a moment later. "Well, it's been fun. I need to get home, though."

He didn't want the time to end. As he tucked the package of pork chops into a fabric bag he'd bought at one of the stalls, he realized he wanted to get to know her better. Figure out why he was reacting to her so strongly. He pointed at the taco truck down the way. "Want to catch dinner before heading back across the river?"

She hesitated, searching his face.

"My treat. As a thank you for showing me the ways of farmers' markets."

Also more, if he were being truthful with himself. Nah. He'd put off the honesty part for later.

"Okay. I can't be gone too much longer, though. I need to get home and milk Pansy."

The goat. How could he forget the goat even for a minute? He smiled at Eden. Hopefully his panic wasn't showing. "The line is moving quickly. Care to chance it?"

"Sure." She fell into step beside him as they wended their way toward the neon green food truck. "They make the best Tex-Mex."

"Good to know." Jacob craned to see the menu posted beside the serving window. "Do you know what you're having?"

"Definitely. The Thai chicken taco."

"Seriously?" He laughed. "Tacos and Thai aren't exactly the same thing."

"I know, but the combo is so good, with the lemongrass. You should give it a try."

He focused on the menu. "I think I'll have the steak taco."

"Chicken."

"Pretty sure it's beef."

Eden swatted his arm lightly. "Funny guy."

He caught her fingers against his arm. "I can be. I can also be very serious."

For a few seconds they gazed into each other's eyes then Eden pulled her hand away and shifted closer to the food truck. "I've seen more serious than funny," she said quietly.

Jacob swallowed hard. "I tend to keep the other side

locked away until I'm comfortable with someone."

She shot him a glance.

What was she thinking? She was so hard to read. And man, he'd all but pinned his heart to his sleeve with that comment. "I'd like to get to know you better. Unless you're seeing someone."

Eden tipped her head and peered at him. "What are you asking?"

"Are you going out with someone?"

Her jaw shifted slightly. "No."

Why was she making this so hard? Or maybe it was him simply bungling the whole thing. It wasn't like he had experience with this sort of thing. "Then I'm wondering if you'd like to hang out some. Get to know each other."

"Are you asking me out?"

Was he? His brain scrambled to catch up. He quirked a grin. "I think I am. But without anything specific in mind at the moment." He touched her back to nudge her forward in the line. They'd be ordering in a minute.

"There's the fine arts show going on this month in various venues." She glanced up at him as though gauging his reaction.

He could do art. It sounded way better than touring a goat farm. "That sounds interesting. All month, you say? Are you free on Saturday?"

"Are you ready to order?"

Jacob turned to the food truck window. "Yes. One steak taco and one Thai chicken taco, please."

The expression on Eden's face proved she didn't know what to think of his invitation. That made two of them. He didn't know, either.

Chapter 7

"NO STINKIN' WAY!" Hailey, her blue eyes gleaming, bounced on the exercise ball at the computer desk in Eden's living room. "You are going out with Jacob Riehl?"

Eden held up her hand. "Once. To the art show."

Hailey bopped her head from side to side. "Eden and Jacob sitting in a tree. K-I-S-S-I-N-G."

"Good grief. That hasn't happened, nor is it likely to."

"But he asked you out. That's wild. I should be jealous, but I think he's too serious for me."

He might prove too serious for Eden, as well. She couldn't believe she'd said yes. She couldn't believe he'd asked. He'd caught her off guard with no ready excuse. Although she was the one who'd suggested the art show. Had she come across as needy?

But there'd been all the times he'd touched her. The brush of his sleeve. The intensity in his eyes. The scent of his aftershave.

"Earth to Eden."

She blinked Hailey back into focus, which was difficult as her friend didn't sit still. "What?"

"What are you going to wear?"

"Clothes."

Hailey rolled her eyes. "It's a hot date. Let me at your closet."

Not a chance. "You're blowing it out of proportion. We're going to an art show. It's casual." Eden gestured at her shirt and shorts. "Something like this will be just fine. Don't worry. I won't go in my milking overalls."

"You said he asked if you were seeing someone else. He's looking for an exclusive."

"That doesn't make it a hot date." Why had she ever confided in Hailey, of all people? She should've known what the inquisition would be like.

"Going out for dinner afterward?"

"He didn't ask."

Hailey leaped from the large ball. "Do I need to go next door and give the man a talking to?"

"Don't you dare. I'll disown you and never speak to you again."

"Then I get twenty-six cinnamon rolls all to myself."

Eden laughed. "You're crazy. Anyway, you're only talking about next door because of Jacob's housemate."

"Well, he is the more fun of the two. No offense."

Logan seemed like a decent enough guy, but he didn't affect her the way Jacob did. Nobody had ever affected her the way he did. She hadn't dated much the past few years, the pain of losing her family all too close to the surface to seek her own happiness.

"You're thinking about your sisters."

Eden blinked at Hailey. “How did you know?”

“You’re running your fingers over that tattoo.”

She hadn’t even noticed. “They’ll never have the chance to date. Get married. Have a family.”

“That’s true, but it’s no reason to pretend those things don’t matter to you.”

Eden surged to her feet and went to the window. Shadows lengthened on the trees beside the river across the street. “Don’t you get it? They’re dead.”

Compassion shone from Hailey’s eyes when Eden turned back. “I know. But you’re not.”

“I should be. I should have been with them.”

“Families don’t always travel together. Especially when the kids are teens and young adults. Listen, Eden. I think the survivor’s guilt thing has been going on long enough. How long has it been?”

“Almost five years,” Eden whispered.

“Just because you’re alive and moving on doesn’t make you a bad sister, a bad daughter. You have to get past it, girl. You have to live today.”

“I don’t know how.” She scooped up the startled cat who’d been napping on the arm of the sofa and hugged him tight. Licorice patted her cheek with one black paw.

“I think you do. You made a start already, agreeing to go out with Jacob. Relax a bit. See where it goes.”

“Why did he even invite me? I know he hates Pansy. Plus, whenever he glances at my tattoo, his eyes kind of narrow. I don’t think he approves.”

Hailey dropped back onto the large ball. “He’s like you. Kind of attracted but not sure why. He’s willing to find out. Honestly, Eden, you’d be crazy to cancel.”

How did her friend know she’d thought of doing just that

in the twenty-four hours since she and Jacob had eaten tacos together at the market? "It's weird. I don't think there's any chance something can come of this. We're too different. He's from a rich family." She waved her hand around her cluttered, shabby living room. "The eighties phoned. They want their ugly carpet back, but I can't afford even a cheap replacement."

"You need to give it back anyway." Hailey's nostrils flared as she looked at the stained, matted gray. "Kass and I put some of that laminate flooring in our apartments above the bakery. It's not that expensive."

"Getting someone to install it doubles the price."

"So we'll do it."

Eden grasped a glimmer of hope. "Did you do yours?" She scratched Licorice's ears and was rewarded with a rumbling purr.

Her friend waved a hand. "No, it was part of what we paid to the contractor. But I watched him for a few minutes. How hard can it be? You just click the rows together across the room."

"Buying the tools would cost as much as hiring someone." It wasn't likely her pink tools were up to the task. She couldn't even whack a nail in with her lightweight hammer. Eden dropped back onto the sofa. "Never mind. We weren't really talking about this house. It needs a ton of work."

Hailey bounced twice then snapped her fingers. "We were talking about two cute guys who already have tools. I bet they'd love to help." She leaned closer. "I'll come, too."

Eden couldn't stifle the laugh that exploded across the room. "There's no cure for the likes of you."

"What?" Hailey put on a wide-eyed innocent look.

"Friends help each other, and we've been friends forever. Besides, if we really do this, you'll need food. I can help with that at least."

"Cinnamon rolls?"

"You have a serious weakness there, girl."

Eden stroked Licorice's back. "I can't deny it."

Hailey surged to her feet and the ball rolled away. "Let me see what you've got to wear. We don't have much time, so if shopping therapy is needed, it's tomorrow after work." She headed toward the staircase.

Eden sprang up. "Wait, no. It's okay. I'll find something."

But nothing deterred Hailey. "I haven't been up here in ages," she said from halfway up. "Remember the sleepovers we used to have?"

Eden slumped onto the sofa, gathering Licorice tighter. Wait for it.

"Eden Andrusek!"

She scrunched her eyes shut.

"This looks exactly like it did when we were in high school." A door shut overhead and footsteps creaked down the hall. "Are you seriously sleeping in your old room when there are two bigger bedrooms available? One of them with a queen-size bed and a door to the bathroom?" Another door opened and closed. "I mean, it has hideous wallpaper, but that can be steamed off."

Was a reply required?

Hailey descended a few steps then sat where she could see Eden. She dropped her chin and stared down. "Girl, this isn't even healthy."

"It's my choice."

"Your parents' clothes are still in their closet. It's been five years."

"So?"

"It's time."

Eden dug her fingers into the cat's back, but Licorice only stretched. "You don't understand."

"It's time, sweetie."

"But..."

"I'll come by with some boxes. We'll figure out what's worth saving—"

"All of it!"

"—and what needs to go. You don't have to do this alone. But it's time."

Was it? Really? Eden found herself nodding. "I guess." Hailey was right. It had just been so easy to postpone, at first from grief then later from guilt. She'd thought — briefly — about tackling the job before, but it seemed so immense avoidance was easier.

Hailey beckoned with her finger. "Now come here and let's find you something to wear on Saturday."

Jacob stood in the front doorway of Eden's house. A black cat twined between her ankles then sauntered across the driveway. "Your cat escaped."

"That's Licorice. He's fine."

She let her cat loose in the neighborhood? Weren't there coyotes and other predators in the wild area next to the river? Whose yard did it use for a litterbox?

Why had he asked her out again? He refocused on her, framed in her doorway, wearing beige capris and a fitted blue top. Right, that's why. Because she was so pretty and really quite nice despite her eccentric ways. And a Christian. "You look terrific." He smiled at her, not at all hard to do. "Are you ready?"

"I just need to grab my purse. Be with you in a sec." She disappeared into the dimly-lit interior.

Jacob strained to see the space. He couldn't see much beyond a gray carpet and blue sofa before she reappeared. A moment later he held the car door for her as she slid into the leather interior. He rounded the car with trembling hands and a pounding head. New territory. He didn't date. He'd sort of had a crush once on a girl in high school, but they'd never gotten beyond a bunch of teens pairing off at youth group events. He'd been too afraid of girls. Too focused on grades.

Jacob pressed the button to start the car in the awkward silence. He glanced at Eden. She sat fiddling with the strap of the purse on her lap. "Where to?"

Her eyes met his and she pointed up the hill. "West on Riverside then north."

"Sounds good." Awkward. What did people talk about on dates, anyway? With someone they barely knew? He shouldn't have attempted this. He could be content alone for the rest of his life, right? No one to mess up his space. No one to leave behind when he jaunted off to Africa with Global Sunbeams for weeks at a time.

"Regretting the invitation?" Eden asked softly. "This doesn't have to be a big deal."

He shot her a glance. She watched him from unreadable blue eyes.

"N-no regrets."

One side of her mouth lifted into a small smile. "You don't sound convinced."

Why couldn't he be suave and confident? Like Logan. Or

even his brothers-in-law. He couldn't imagine either Gabe or Keanan being completely tongue-tied in the presence of a woman. He should have practiced up.

Jacob rearranged his hands on the steering wheel. His fingers hurt from the clenching. "It's just that I've never done this before."

"Art shows don't usually set off panic attacks."

"I've been to art shows."

She gave a little snicker.

Jacob stiffened, but a sidelong glance revealed fun, not derision, dancing in her eyes. Relax, Riehl. One date isn't going to kill you. You don't ever have to do this again if you don't want to. "I haven't ever dated."

In his periphery, he saw her head tip to one side. "Never ever?"

He shook his head. "Not even once."

"Let me guess. Too busy with chess club?"

"I quit chess club at the request of my principal."

"Oh? I'd have thought you'd be good at that sort of thing."

"I am."

"Then...?"

Jacob sighed. "Nobody wanted to play against me because I beat them all so quickly, okay? I didn't mind leaving the club. They weren't a challenge."

Eden shifted so she was all but facing him in the passenger seat. "Wow. You are more of a geek than I thought."

What was that supposed to mean? Insult or compliment? He'd pretend compliment until proven otherwise. He'd scare her off sooner or later, anyway. It might as well be sooner and save them both some trouble. "Do you play chess?"

"I'd never admit it if I did. Not now."

He couldn't help the grin. "You didn't answer my question."

Her fingers stroked her tattoo. "My dad tried to teach my sisters and me. I didn't take to it."

The opening he'd been waiting for. "What does your tattoo represent?"

Eden's hands clenched in her lap and her jaw tightened.

Uh oh. Wrong question. He barely heard her whispered reply. "My family."

He hadn't meant to cause her pain. "How so? Are they… gone?"

She sucked in her lower lip and nodded. Her eyes filled with unshed tears.

There. A quiet side street. Jacob veered around the corner, parked, and shut off the car. He angled toward her from the driver's seat. "Tell me what happened? If you want to. If it will help."

Her jaw worked for a few seconds before she gave a terse nod, blinking quickly. "Five years ago. They were going to my Baba's seventy-fifth birthday over in Ritzville."

"Baba?"

"My grandmother. My father's mother."

"Okay. What happened?" Something major must have by the devastation on her face. When she hesitated a moment longer, Jacob reached across the console and covered her fidgeting fingers with his.

"They... had an accident on I-90." Her voice broke. "They ended up under a semi in the next lane. My parents, both sisters, gone just like that." She pulled her hands away and brought them up to her cover her face, her shoulders shaking with silent sobs.

He wasn't good at this sort of thing, but he couldn't just sit here and do nothing. Not when he was responsible for the breakdown. Jacob rounded the car, opened the door, and pulled Eden out and into his arms. "Cry."

Not that she needed his invitation. She leaned against him, soaking his shirt with her tears.

Jacob rested his cheek against the top of her head and rubbed both hands across her back. He hoped it was half as comforting for her as it was for him.

Chapter 8

I'M SORRY FOR BLUBBERING all over you." Eden set her hands on Jacob's upper arms and tried to push out of his hold.

His hands caught behind her back, giving her a bit of space. Enough space to look up at him. That might have been a mistake. Compassion filled his blue eyes. "I'm sorry for pushing you to tell me."

She'd bet he was. "I'm okay now. Really." She blinked rapidly to get rid of the last few tears and pulled a smile from somewhere. "See?"

"I can't imagine losing everyone I loved in one nanosecond."

"Be glad you don't have to." Eden sniffled, brushing at her face with her forearm.

Jacob pulled a neatly folded handkerchief out of his pocket and offered it to her.

This was her escape. She took a few steps away and blew her nose. "Thanks. I'll wash it and get it back to you."

He glanced around. "Want to walk?"

Weren't they on their way to the art show? Here they were in a residential neighborhood not far from the community college, only halfway to their destination. Oh, what did the art show matter, anyway? It was open all of June. She could go another time. It wasn't as though she could afford to buy anything. She jerked her head in a nod and started down the sidewalk.

A beep behind her signaled that Jacob had locked the car. Hands buried in his pockets, he fell into step beside her, sleeve brushing against her arm. The other night he'd kept touching her back. A few minutes ago he'd held her while she cried. Talk about mixed messages. He said he'd never dated, but he should know something about women. He had sisters.

So had she, once.

She took a deep breath. "I never answered your question."

Eden sensed him looking at her but didn't turn.

"It's okay. I don't need to know."

"No. It's not a secret. After I got through the first crush of grief, I decided to get this tattoo. There are four roses, one for each of them, so I'll never forget. The pain I endured was nothing compared to what happened to them."

Jacob stopped in the middle of the sidewalk and turned toward her, his eyes focused on her arm. "May I?"

Might he what? But it couldn't be too horrible if he was asking. She nodded.

His fingers slowly traced each of the four roses.

Goosebumps rose at his gentle contact. She shivered.

Immediately his eyes swung to meet hers. "I'm sorry."

Eden swallowed hard. "It's okay. No one has ever touched it before." Not like that, for sure.

"It's a beautiful remembrance."

"Do you mean that?" She'd seen the way he'd looked at

her tattoo before. Definitely not as though it were a thing of beauty.

"I do." His hands captured both of hers. "It makes sense to me."

I do. The traditional marriage vow. Eden held her breath, staring deep into Jacob's eyes. Was she losing her heart to this man? She couldn't be. Not to someone who valued order as much as he did. Who was so uptight. But didn't love bring out the best in everyone? She and Pansy had barged into his life without a proper introduction. No wonder he'd withdrawn. She should be thankful he offered her a second chance.

His gaze dropped to her lips.

Wasn't it too soon for a kiss? They barely knew each other.

Jacob gave her hands a squeeze and let go, taking a step back. He angled his head. "Let's walk."

The moment was gone. Probably a good thing, really, but the sense of disappointment lingered. They walked half a block in silence. This was crazy. Eden reached for his hand and threaded her fingers between his. She could live without kissing, at least for now, but she needed his touch. Needed to know this new relationship was real and not just her imagination. If it might, someday, transcend friendship.

His fingers tightened around hers as they ambled down the sidewalk. "Thanks," he whispered.

She peered up at him. "For what?"

"For this." Jacob swung their joined hands out in front of them. "I don't know how to do this dating thing, Eden. But I'm willing to learn."

"I don't really know how to do it, either." She leaned closer until their arms pressed against each other. "But I'm willing to learn with you."

He smiled at her, eyes warm and inviting. "Is this when I tell you I like you?"

Eden grinned back. "It sounds like it might be. So I'll set your mind at ease. I like you, too."

"I'm glad we've got that settled." Humor laced his words, but she heard the relief behind them.

"Me, too."

"So what do we do now?"

"I think this is the stage where we spend time together and get to know each other. Find out if a friendship is enough." Oh, man. Her mouth was running off.

Jacob nodded. "So you know, I don't see myself dating just for fun. I mean, I expect to have fun..." His voice trailed off.

"Me, too. I'm not like Hailey—"

"Thank goodness," he whispered.

Eden grinned. "She loves to play the field. I mean, she wants to settle down someday, of course." Hailey would kill her if she got wind of this conversation. What if Hailey and Logan ended up together? Eden didn't want to be responsible for scaring Logan off. "When she meets the right guy."

"Okay. So we date for a while. Get to know each other. See where it goes." Jacob nodded. "Sounds good. I like the sound of it."

Could she really do this with a man who needed to map out their entire relationship when it had barely begun? Must be the chess player in him, always looking half a dozen moves ahead. "There's always the possibility it won't last," she said slowly. "Not trying to jinx anything. Just saying that's something we need to stay aware of. We might have a big fight we can't get past." Like maybe about Pansy. That was a distinct possibility.

Jacob's fingers tightened around hers. "But we won't give up easily. We'll talk to each other, right? We'll try to clear it up before it gets too big to manage. I've seen what happens when people don't talk. My sister Sierra kept some major stuff from Gabe when they were dating. They almost didn't survive that. She shouldn't have held back but trusted him to help her work through it."

Eden's mind flashed back to her few months at Green Acres Farm, remembering Sierra and Gabe's joy as they prepared to welcome their first adopted child into their home. What could possibly have been the big issue? Not that it was any of her business. She nodded. "We'll talk. I promise. I'll probably talk so much I'll send you running from that alone."

"I don't think so. I like the sound of your voice. It's like music."

She nudged him. "Wow, Jacob Riehl. I don't think anyone has ever said anything nicer to me in my life. My sister Indigo used to say I screeched like an owl."

He shook his head. "Not a chance."

Jacob couldn't wipe the grin off his face as he opened the door. A crescendo of piano music assaulted him. He stood in the doorway and let the praise song wash over him, adding its joy and triumph to his own.

Did God approve of his new relationship with Eden? Surely He did. God had orchestrated their meeting, right down to that silly goat. Jacob had finished the presentation in time and gotten the contract anyway, so he could forgive

Pansy. Someday they'd look back on the goat and laugh about how she'd caused them to meet.

"That you, Jacob?" Logan called out over the music.

"Yes." Jacob entered the front hall, took off his shoes, and arranged them neatly beside Logan's before coming around into the living room.

Logan's eyebrows rose into his hair as his fingers continued to run over the keys. "So how was the hot date?"

Jacob felt his grin wobble. "It wasn't a hot date. It was a first date. And it was good."

His friend laughed. "First dates can be hot, too, for the record. How was the art show? See anything you needed to have?"

Only Eden. Jacob shook his head. "We never made it to the art show."

The music stopped in mid-measure as Logan's hands froze. "Oh?"

"We got talking and went for a walk instead."

The melody for Here Comes the Bride poured out of the keyboard.

Jacob flushed. "Not so fast."

"Did you kiss her?"

"Of course not."

"This I've got to hear," muttered Logan under his breath. "Why not?"

"It's too soon." Jacob frowned. "We just met, and this was the first time we went out."

"Lots of guys kiss a girl goodnight on the doorstep after the first date." Logan glanced at the large window overlooking the back yard. "On the other hand, it's broad daylight."

Jacob settled on the arm of the leather sofa. "Would you kiss a girl on the first date?" Had Eden expected him to? Had he blown protocol already? He hadn't held back because he didn't want to, that was for sure.

"I have done so." Logan bent his head, hair hiding his face, as he pounded out another song.

"Did you regret it?"

"Kind of." His roommate glanced over, a lopsided grin on his face. "I mean, none of them worked out, right? But it's not that big a deal. A kiss isn't like a diamond ring. It's not a promise."

Jacob crossed his arms. "I don't want to kiss a bunch of different women." Although he really did want to kiss Eden. Just the thought gave him sweaty palms and butterflies in his stomach. He couldn't imagine going through that, sharing that level of intimacy, and then not marrying her.

"Then don't." Logan leaned over the keyboard as he slowed the tempo and switched to The Love of God.

Jacob felt the melodies pour over him, the lyrics seeping into his soul. The love of God. How rich and pure. How measureless and strong. If he couldn't feel that kind of love for Eden, at least as much as any man could feel for a woman, he didn't deserve to kiss her.

Eden crouched beside the goat stand and stripped the last of the milk from Pansy's udder. "I'm sorry I left you alone all day. I can't help it on days I have to work, but this is Saturday."

"Maa."

She wasn't really sorry. Not until she'd seen Pansy's discomfort at a late milking. If she was going to go on dates — and she was, right? — how could she manage the chores? Pansy needed relief every twelve hours, and the morning milking couldn't be moved much due to starting work at eight. In the dark mornings of winter, Eden could barely drag herself out of bed for that six-thirty rendezvous. It wasn't reasonable to try to move it earlier, and later wasn't an option.

No, she'd make it work. She had to. Pansy's needs had to come first, even if it meant coming home earlier, like she should've today, or going out for a later dinner after chores. If Jacob was the right man for her, he'd understand and help her work around Pansy's schedule.

She picked up the milk bucket then wrapped her other arm around the goat. "Want to come play in the yard for a while? I'll take this inside then I need to clean the chickens' water tower."

"Maa."

Licorice twined between Eden's ankles before jumping on the stand and rubbing Pansy's legs. The goat butted the cat, but he wasn't that easy to budge.

Eden chuckled. "Come on, you two."

Pansy bounded into the backyard ahead of her, but Licorice leaped from the railing around the goat pen roof to an overhanging tree. He strolled down the limb and hopped onto the fence dividing her yard from Jacob and Logan's. Then he disappeared.

What would Jacob think of her cat visiting him? Hopefully it would be fine. If they were to have a future together, he'd need to accept she wasn't a goldfish-for-pets kind of woman.

Chapter 9

JACOB HAD MEANT TO CALL Eden and ask if she'd like to ride to church with him and Logan, but he didn't have her phone number. And how would it work, anyway? Whose car would they take? Who would sit in the backseat? Not Eden.

He'd gone over and, unable to find a doorbell, knocked on her door. There'd been no answer, though her car was in the driveway. He could hear Pansy out back but, with no desire to see the goat again, he'd returned home. When he'd next looked out, her car was gone.

Okay. They'd ease into this whole relationship thing. It was better that way anyway. He and Logan arrived at Bridgeview Bible Church about ten minutes before the service was due to start and, palms sweating, he looked around for Eden.

She stood in the foyer, chatting and laughing with several other young women, Hailey among them.

Jacob hesitated. He wasn't ready to brave that particular friend.

"Good morning!" The pastor's wife reached out to shake his hand. "Jacob, isn't it? Welcome back."

"That's right. Good to be here."

"Hi, Juanita." Smiling, Logan nodded at the woman. "We're happy to be back. We enjoyed Pastor Tomas's message last week."

Not as much as Jacob had enjoyed catching glimpses of Eden across the small sanctuary. Forgive me, Lord. Sunday morning should be all about worshiping God. But that didn't quite make sense, either. Wasn't Jesus supposed to be the most important every minute? Which didn't mean no other relationship mattered.

A movement across the foyer caught his eye and he looked up to meet Eden's smile as several of her friends strolled through the sanctuary doors, still chatting.

He grinned back, raising his eyebrows slightly.

Aw, she looked a bit shy. Like she wasn't sure what to do now, either. "Excuse me, please." Jacob stepped around Logan and approached Eden. "Would you like to sit with me?" Man, she was gorgeous in that pretty sleeveless dress that swirled just above her knees. Her hair cascaded to her shoulders. She smelled amazing, like a spring morning.

Her fingers tangled with his before he quite knew what was happening. "Sure."

"Your friends won't mind?"

"We can sit with them. Or not. Whatever you like."

Jacob glanced into the sanctuary just as Hailey looked over her shoulder and winked at him. Aw, man. What was he supposed to do with that? Surely it was on Eden's behalf.

"Don't mind Hailey," Eden whispered. "She knows about us. She'll leave you alone."

It looked like Hailey had left three seats. Jacob took a deep breath. "Okay." He leaned closer to Eden. "Have I told you how beautiful you are?"

She cast him a startled look. "Th-thanks. Ready?"

He nodded and kept a firm grip on her hand. She preceded him up the aisle then slid in beside Hailey.

Logan settled into the aisle seat a few seconds later. "Nice work," he whispered, nudging Jacob.

Pastor Tomas took the podium. "If you'll open your hymnals to number two-ninety-four, we'll get started. Francesca phoned a few minutes ago to say her allergies flared up so badly she can't come this morning and play for us, so you're stuck with me. But the Lord wants us to come and worship, no matter how polished our coming."

Jacob flipped to the correct hymn. The Love of God. He glanced at Logan, but his friend was already rising as he eyed the baby grand beside the small platform.

Logan stepped into the aisle. "Need a pianist, pastor? I'll be happy to play if I know the songs."

Tomas motioned toward the piano. "If you are capable of bringing music from that piece of furniture, please do."

Logan moved the piano bench back a few inches as he took a seat. His fingers flowed over the keys as he pounded out the introduction. Tomas missed the entry point, as did most of the congregation. Those that had started quickly petered out. Logan played through the chorus and came back around, watching the pastor more closely this time. Then, seeming to come to a decision, he began to sing.

Around Jacob, voices joined in the century-old hymn.

"Wow," Eden whispered, tugging him close enough to hear. "Can he ever play."

Jacob grinned, pride for his buddy swelling his chest. "He can. Music is his life."

"It's amazing." Then she turned forward and closed her eyes for a few seconds before joining in.

Jacob sang along, too. He definitely wasn't in Logan's league, but he could carry a tune well enough not to embarrass himself. Well enough to praise the Lord. Hearing Eden lift her voice beside him warmed him to the core of his being. Wasn't this love of Jesus the most important thing they could have in common?

Eden cringed when she saw Marietta Santoro making her way through the crowded foyer after church, a speculative gleam in the eyes trained on her and Jacob. But it was too late to remove her hand from where it was tucked in Jacob's. Half the congregation had probably noticed by now. A good number had given her a grin, a wink, or a thumbs-up. She'd attended this church most of her life, and folks had always had her best interest at heart, especially after the loss of her family.

"Eden Andrusek!" Marietta crushed Eden's face between both her hands. "Is it true? You are turning away from my Roberto for this newcomer? Jacob, he seems a nice boy, si, but he is not a Santoro. He did not grow up in Bridgeview."

The pressure on her cheeks made it hard for Eden to smile at the elderly Italian woman. Dating someone who hadn't been born within six blocks of her house seemed like a positive at the moment. "Marietta, you know Rob and I didn't hit it off."

"My Antonio will be returning soon to open a restaurant. He would be good for you, tesoro. A little younger than you, perhaps, but not so much."

Eden didn't feel like Marietta's treasure at the moment.

More like her target. She clung to Jacob's hand. "Thanks for caring, Marietta. I should thank you for renting your extra house to Jacob and Logan."

Marietta's hands flew into the air, to Eden's relief. "I knew I should not have let strangers into the neighborhood. First we take care of our own, si?"

"Yes, thank you for renting to us." Jacob pressed against her arm as he leaned toward the conversation. "It's a great little house in a terrific location." He paused. "Right across from the river. A bit of nature in the middle of the city."

"What do you know of nature? Portland is bigger than Spokane. Such a city."

"Nonna, don't be silly." Jasmine took her grandmother's arm. "There is nature everywhere if a person just looks for it. It's not Jacob's fault he was raised in Portland. Give him a chance. If Eden likes him, he must be a good guy, okay? Leave her be already."

Marietta shrugged Jasmine away. "But Roberto, he is a bene man."

Jasmine rolled her eyes. "Rob is full of himself, Nonna. He needs to grow up a little before any decent woman will look twice."

Her grandmother glared at her. "Do not speak ill of your cousin. And do not decide to fall in love with the other newcomer." She spared a narrowed glance in Logan's direction.

Eden heard Logan stifle a chuckle behind her.

"At least you won't try to marry me off to a Santoro cousin, Nonna. I'll marry whom I choose, even if he is not Italian." Jasmine's gaze swept Logan up and down. "Maybe not that one, although God's music does flow from his fingertips. Didn't you enjoy the piano this morning?"

A strangled sound from Logan caught Eden's attention.

"Francesca—" began Marietta.

"Cannot play like that, Nonna. You know it. She does well enough, but she doesn't have the talent in both hands he has in his baby finger. Just admit you enjoyed the music."

"It was rather loud."

"Admit it."

Marietta threw her hands up. "Fine. It was acceptable. But mark my words, those boys—" she glared from one to the other "—will be gone anytime. Their kind always moves on."

Jacob found his voice. "We did sign a one-year lease, Marietta. We're not going anywhere anytime soon."

The old woman wagged a finger in Eden's face. "Mark my words. He'll be gone, leaving you with a broken heart."

"Enough, Nonna." Jasmine grasped her grandmother's arm. "You are coming for Sunday dinner, si? Mamma has lasagna in the oven."

Marietta sniffed. "She makes it like an American."

"We are American. Come along, Nonna." As she all but dragged the older woman away, Jasmine met Eden's gaze and mouthed sorry.

Eden shook her head slightly and grinned.

"Wow." Jacob broke the sudden silence. "She's something else."

"Please pardon Marietta Santoro." Pastor Tomas closed the gap. "She lends distinctive flavor to our congregation. Also, thank you, Logan, for filling in this morning."

"Anytime, pastor. Though I don't wish to step on anyone's toes."

Tomas waved a hand. "Francesca will be glad to have someone to share the duty with. She is not her grandmother."

Eden turned to Logan. "Your playing was amazing. I

could listen to it all day."

Jacob nudged her. "Should I be worried?"

She tapped a finger to her cheek, pretending to think. "Well..." She tightened her grip with her other hand. "Probably not."

"Whew."

Logan grinned at her. "Thanks, Eden."

Tomas looked between them. "I simply wish to say we are happy to have you at Bridgeview Bible and hope you will consider making this your church home. Whether it is for a short time—" his gaze lingered on Eden "—or for many years, we would be blessed."

Jacob let go of her hand just long enough to firmly shake Tomas's. "Thank you, pastor. I appreciated your message this morning."

Juanita stepped up beside Tomas and took his arm. "I'd planned to invite you men to lunch today if you attended again." Her gaze landed on Eden. "You're welcome to come, too, if you like."

Eden felt her head shaking before she'd made a conscious decision. "Thanks, but no. I didn't get my weekend chores done yesterday, so I'd better not."

Jacob's gaze pierced her cheek, but she didn't turn. It was true, after all. Saturday had always been her catch-up day. How was she going to fit dating Jacob into her life on a regular basis? She didn't need to look at him to remember his expressive blue eyes or curly blond hair. To remember his earnest expression and his halting words as he asked if they could date. He was worth fitting in. Maybe in time he'd help her care for Pansy and the chickens to allow more time for them to spend together.

"What do you think, Jacob?" asked Logan across her.

"Did you have any other plans?"

"No, that sounds great, Juanita. Thanks for the invitation. Can we bring anything?"

"Not at all. Everything is covered. Tomas can give you directions to the house while I make sure things are put away here." She turned and left the foyer.

Jacob tugged her aside as Logan and Tomas conferred. "You okay?" he whispered, facing her and taking both her hands.

She met his gaze. "I'm fine. I really do have things I need to do." Is this where she reminded him she was an introvert? She needed downtime. Time to process.

"I'm sorry I took you away from your chores yesterday."

"Don't be. I had a good time." She gave him a cautious smile. He didn't really regret it, did he? "But I do have to clean the pens and do some laundry. You have a good time at Tomas and Juanita's. She's a good cook."

His thumbs traced circles on the backs of her hands. "When can I see you again?"

Anytime. We live next door. But that was a flippant answer to a different question. She needed to take this relationship slowly. "We could do the night market again on Wednesday, if you like."

"Can I pick you up?" A look of chagrin crossed his face. "I don't even know where your office is. If you even work out of one."

"In the public works building near Riverfront Square. It's just a five-minute bike ride to Kendall Yards from there so, unless you have a bike rack on your car, it's easier to meet at the market." Eden tipped her head. "I could send you a text if I happened to be out on a call." She pulled out her cell.

He raised his eyebrows. “Get many complaints on miscreant goats?”

Was he trying to be funny, or was he serious? “Not as many as you might think. Where is your office?”

“Not far from the Steam Plant. You’re sure it’s okay to meet at the market?” He quirked a grin. “That doesn’t sound very date-like.” He dug out his cell and they exchanged numbers.

“It’s good, for this week at least.” Wow, now that she had the full attention of his intense eyes, Eden regretted saying she wouldn’t join them for lunch. But she couldn’t change her mind. Her reasons were valid. Plus, she did need the distance to think clearly.

“Okay.” Jacob leaned closer and swept his lips across her forehead. “I’ll talk to you soon.”

She stood, dazed, as he moved away.

Chapter 10

"YOU SURE YOU DON'T want to go down to Riverfront Park for the day?" Jacob paused, ready to shut his car trunk on the lunch Eden had packed into a picnic basket.

Beautiful as always, she swung to meet his gaze. "Do you? There will be a lot of people." She'd braided her hair from her forehead back, though some red-gold tendrils had already escaped.

"I don't want to disappoint you if that's what you've always done on the fourth of July. Do you usually take part in all the festivities? I hear there's an arts and crafts show, and we never did get to the art show that day two weeks ago."

Eden shrugged. "I'll go if you want to, but the whole event is not really my thing. I get enough of people every day at work."

He could finally exhale. "If you're sure."

"Totally. I'm surprised you'd ask, though. You're even more of an introvert than I am, and that's saying something."

Jacob reached for her hands and tugged her close. "I'd rather spend the day with you than with five thousand other people."

"That's a conservative estimate," she murmured against his chest, sliding her arms around him. "I'd rather go hiking with you."

"Then it's a good thing that's our plan. Mount Spokane State Park, here we come!"

She felt so good in his arms, like she fit, somehow. But wasn't that a bit crazy? Not if God made her for you. Great. Now he was hearing voices. Jacob dropped his hands and took a step back, inhaling sharply. He opened the car door for Eden then rounded the vehicle and slid in the driver's seat. "You'll have to give me directions."

She flashed him a grin. "I'm good at that. Everyone needs their talents."

"And here I thought it was one of mine." He put the car into Reverse. "Which way, direction giver?"

Eden's face flushed. "North on Division Street Bridge."

"You've got it. Wow, I hope you don't micromanage people at work that much."

She swung to look at him. "What do you mean?"

"Teasing. You're giving this newcomer the freedom to find the bridge and go north without interference. Are you sure that's wise?"

"Do you know where Division is?" She narrowed her eyes.

Jacob kept the smirk hidden. "Yes."

"How about the river? And the direction north?"

"I think I can handle that."

"Then I don't know what you're complaining about."

"Want to do dinner at The Oyster when we get back into

the city? He glanced at her. “We can go straight to the park from there for the fireworks.”

She gave him an unreadable look. “I need to milk Pansy around six-thirty.”

The thought of the goat soured his mood just a little. Would they ever get to have a day out without catering to the animal?

Eden leaned back in the seat and closed her eyes.

Jacob would’ve thought having two sisters would help him understand Eden, but there didn’t seem to be any evidence to support that. He hadn’t overly cared about figuring them out. They were just a bossy part of his life as a kid. Eden was different. He actually wanted to see her bright and happy, but accomplishing it consistently seemed as likely as vacationing on Mars.

She avoided looking at him all the way down West Main. He stopped at Browne as southbound traffic flowed by. “You been into Main Market Co-op?” he asked, his attention caught by the solar panels on the roof and the huge mural facing them across the intersection.

“It’s where I shop.”

The bright mural was covered with images of food. And a goat. Of course, she’d been in there. “They must supply their own power from the solar panels.”

Eden glanced his way. That was something at least. “They do.”

The light turned green. After hanging a left onto Division, they crossed the bridge. Jacob relaxed. They’d be on this divided highway for miles before the next turn. He could focus his attention back to the silent woman in the passenger seat.

“Did I say something wrong?” He’d never dreamed he’d

be the guy who asked that question. He'd heard his brothers-in-law joke about getting the low-down from his sisters. Women always said it was—

"Nothing's wrong."

Warning bells went off in Jacob's head. Hadn't Sierra's husband, Gabe, said it was never nothing? That the word was a woman's code for the guy being an insensitive jerk? Jacob sent his mind back over the past half hour. She'd seemed fine at first, not only accepting his hug but returning it. But once he asked her for dinner, she'd cooled right off.

"You seem rather quiet," he ventured.

"I'm okay." She rubbed her temples. "I seem to have a bit of a headache, though."

"There's Advil in the glove box."

"No, I'll be fine. It's not that bad."

"Eden, I'm no expert with women." Now there was an understatement sure to win an award. He forged ahead. "But I'm pretty sure I'm being punished for something, and I don't know what." He hadn't even reacted to her words about the goat. "Help a guy out here?"

"I'm not sure how we're going to work out, Jacob. We're just too different."

"We're supposed to be different, aren't we?" He glanced over just as she narrowed a gaze at him.

"I didn't mean the guy-girl thing."

It might be a good thing they had the whole day of hiking in front of them. It could take that long to finish one conversation. Why couldn't she just say what she meant instead of what she didn't? He'd play along for now. "Then what?"

"You're a rich kid, and I'm really, really not. I mean, compare this car to mine."

The sleek hybrid BMW had been a graduation gift from his parents. Her car had rusty fenders. Point taken. "We had the same vehicles last week. If it bothered you then, you didn't mention it."

She crossed her arms in front of her then uncrossed them. "And, well, you hate Pansy."

"I don't hate her." Exactly.

"I'm really sorry she ate your papers. I'm really sorry that's how we met."

"I'm over it, Eden. I got the presentation done and nailed the contract for the community center. It's okay."

"But you still hate her."

Jacob blew out an exasperated breath. "Hate is a rather strong word."

She crossed her arms again. "What would you call it, then?"

"Eden, why are we talking about your goat? I'm not dating her. I'm dating you." He shot her a glance. "Unless you're having second thoughts?"

"Are you?"

"What, me?" Man, why was he driving right now? He needed to be able to hold her, hug her, maybe even kiss her. Except he hadn't gone there yet. Jacob reached across the console and tugged her hand free. He rubbed his thumb over her hand on her knee. "Eden, I am so not having second thoughts. I really like you, and I want to get to know you better."

"Pansy's part of my life, Jacob."

A part that would be gone when they got married and lived in one of those Leeds-approved condos in Kendall Yards. The city didn't allow livestock over there. Whoa. His brain was miles ahead. Or maybe down a rabbit trail.

"I know." He didn't like it, but he was fully aware.

"Just so you don't forget."

He squeezed her fingers. "No forgetting. I promise." An easy pledge to fulfill. The goat made her presence known from the "maa" he could hear from his own yard to the effect it had on Eden's schedule. No, he couldn't forget the goat even if he tried.

Eden leaned back against Jacob's chest where they sat on the grass overlooking Riverfront Park, his arms wrapped around her. She could get used to this.

They'd had a great hike and picnic. Things had loosened up, and she'd shoved her misgivings about Pansy into a back corner. The subject wasn't over by any means, but he would come around. She couldn't think of any other possibility, or she was completely wasting her time dating him.

It wasn't just time. With every lingering look, every swing of their joined hands, every crooked smile from his gorgeous face, she lost a tiny piece of her heart. And now this. Wrapped entirely in his embrace, feeling his cheek against hers as they waited for the fireworks to start.

The real kind, not the verbal sparks nor the emotional ones. Just honest-to-goodness colorful explosions in the sky above.

"Have I told you you're beautiful?" he whispered into her ear.

"You may have mentioned it." She let out a deep sigh. No one else ever had, not even in passing, let alone several times a day. She was totally falling in love with this man.

So he didn't like Pansy. He'd get over it. And he couldn't help being a rich kid. Why had she flung that at him, anyway? She was doing okay. Making ends meet.

Hailey was right, though. Enough with hanging onto the guilt. She'd left the shrine up long enough. She really needed to take care of her family's clothes and personal items. Then she could step forward into her future.

Jacob nuzzled her neck, and her insides did funny things.

The first boom exploded into its colorful display, and several more followed in quick succession. A visual for what her stomach felt like when she was near Jacob.

Eden had never been so unaware of fireworks blasting her eardrums and arcing across the night sky right in front of her. Her whole being focused on the dozens of points of contact between her body and Jacob's, especially her shoulder and neck where his chin and cheek rested.

This was good, right? He was a believer. Into sustainability and real food. Everything else could be worked out. She nudged the image of Pansy that floated into her mind aside. She tipped her head slightly so she could look up at him.

His eyes looked even bluer as an immense blue explosion peppered the sky. He was watching her, not the fireworks.

Eden reached up and traced his jaw, feeling it tense beneath her exploring fingertips.

Jacob caught her hand and pressed it against his face then brought it to his lips, his eyes never leaving hers. He branded her palm with a succession of feathery kisses that sent shivers clear to her toes.

That wasn't enough. Not nearly enough. She twisted more, lifting her face to his. His eyes asked a question as the sky darkened, and she stretched closer in reply. His fingers caught in her hair as he drew her face to his, his warm lips meeting hers gently.

She couldn't let him pull away. Not yet. Not until she'd replied. And reply she did, teasing his lips with hers until his hands tightened around her, and he deepened the kiss.

The fourth of July celebration had nothing on this. Her lips became the center of her universe as the fireworks arced out to tingle her entire body. Breathing was optional.

Far too soon, Jacob pulled away and rested his cheek against her face. "Wow," he whispered, his breath sweet on hers.

With no more fireworks in the sky, the park lights kicked back into action. People chattered as they gathered blankets and lawn chairs and made their way back to their vehicles. A small child cried. Car doors slammed. Motors started.

Still Eden sat cocooned in Jacob's embrace, her entire being wrapped in his arms. He cushioned her head against his shoulder, and she rested a moment. Secure.

"I should get you home."

She shook her head against his neck.

"I know, sweetheart. I know." He chuckled softly. "But we have as long as we need." He pressed a kiss to her temple and released her. "Come on."

Apparently the moment was over. It was for the best. She knew that, but it didn't mean she had to like it.

He clambered to his feet and held out his hand. When he'd pulled her upright, he tucked her tight against his side and started for the sidewalk amid the crowd.

Eden could get used to this.

Chapter 11

THE AROMA OF SIZZLING Italian sausage greeted Jacob as he came in the front door. "Smells amazing." He placed his sport sandals in the hall closet before entering the kitchen.

Logan looked up from the stove. "I figured it was time for a home-cooked meal around here."

Was that some kind of jab? Yeah, Jacob had ordered in pretty often in the past couple of weeks since he'd spent so much time with Eden, but he'd always been home for supper. Pansy took priority this time of day in Eden's life, so he'd focused on after-work walks and weekend afternoon dates. What guy had ever given over for a goat before?

Logan poured a jar of pasta sauce into the pot.

"Thought you said home-cooked."

"Cooked by Marietta. She flagged me down on my way home from work this afternoon to talk about a little project."

"Oh?" Jacob set a roll of construction blueprints on the peninsula and slid onto a stool. "Sounds ominous."

Logan chuckled. "You never know with Marietta. She wants to turn that empty lot next to her house into a community garden."

"Doesn't everyone have their own? I mean, if they want one."

"Not everyone has a flat enough space or good light." Logan pointed his wooden spoon at the kitchen window. "Even this place isn't ideal what with the rock bluff on the south side of our yard."

Jacob shrugged. "I guess. There's good fresh food at Main Market Co-op, though, and the farmers' markets."

"A lot of people like growing their own. Anyway, Marietta asked if I'd be willing to construct a fence around the yard and some garden beds in my spare time. She's got a gal named Linnea doing the over all landscaping."

Something about that sounded fishy. "Is she paying you?"

Logan shook his head. "No. I was voluntold."

"You can always say no." Jacob studied his friend. "Tell me that's what you said."

"No way. I've been bored. I need to get out and do things. If she gives me more jars of pasta sauce, that's as good as money. Maybe I'll even try my hand at growing some vegetables."

"She's just trying to set you up with Jasmine."

"Maybe. She has a passel of other grandkids, too, though." Logan chuckled. "It doesn't matter. Marietta can't make me fall in love with Jasmine. She's nice enough, but no spark."

Jacob had sparks with Eden. All kinds of them, but mostly good. "Isn't mid-July the wrong time of year to build a garden?" He might not have a lot of personal experience, but the gang at Green Acres had been busy seeding when he'd visited at the end of May.

"She said something about planting a few fall crops. Also that if it's all done now, it will be ready in springtime."

"You sound like you're considering sticking around when our lease is up."

Logan glanced over as he stirred the sauce. "I kind of like Bridgeview. The whole neighborhood, I mean. There's a good vibe going on."

"Been to Kendall Yards?" Jacob unrolled the blueprints and anchored one end with the fruit basket.

"For the market." Logan brought the wooden spoon to his lips and blew on it before tasting. "Wow, good sauce."

"Across the river is the place to live. The whole development is being built around green principles and developing an intentional community."

"Dude, we've got that right here. You've been to a couple of neighborhood meetings. These people know each other and look out for each other."

Jacob grinned. "At least Marietta. She keeps an eye on everyone." He'd seen her watching a few times when he and Eden had driven by. She'd waved from her porch, but he wasn't sure she approved.

"Right. Marietta. Her husband's been gone about ten years now. His name was Salvador. They both grew up in Bridgeview."

"Why does that not surprise me?"

"What's gotten into you, Jacob? You never used to be this cynical. I always heard a man in love went floating through life, but I'm not seeing it. If being with Eden makes you this grumpy, you should break up with her."

Jacob reared back. "I'm happy. I think she's the one, you know?"

Logan turned the burner down then leaned against the counter next to the stove, facing Jacob with his arms crossed. "But."

"But nothing." Everything was terrific except for the goat and, if he were to be perfectly honest, the chickens, though they were easier to ignore. Livestock belonged on a farm like Green Acres, not in the city. Thankfully not every neighborhood allowed them. Kendall Yards, for instance.

"I still say but."

"Whatever. I think I love Eden, and I think she loves me back. She's sweet and funny." And kissed rather well, not that Jacob had anyone to compare that with. "I'm trying not to rush things with her. In my belief system, marriage is for life, so I want to make really sure."

"Marriage, huh?"

"Okay, so we've only known each other a month. That's what I mean. A few weeks isn't long enough to leap into a lifelong commitment."

"And yet you're thinking about it."

"I'm twenty-six, man. Pretty sure it's okay to be looking for the right woman to marry. To settle down with. Have kids."

"I still say there's a but in there somewhere."

Jacob glared at Logan. Since when did his best friend figure he knew more about Jacob's love life than he did himself?

"I think there's another woman."

"What? You have definitely gone off the deep end. I've never dated anyone in my life before."

Logan waggled his eyebrows. "I think her name is Pansy."

Oh. "Don't be an idiot." Even to his own ears, that sounded weak.

"You're playing second fiddle to a goat. Bet that irks."

The silence went on a little too long as he tried to figure

out a casual response. He came up empty.

"Nailed it in one." Logan gave the sauce another stir then dipped a pasta scoop into a larger pot on the other burner. He pinched a piece of spaghetti between his thumb and forefinger. "Perfect. You hungry?"

He had been. "I'll get the salad out." Jacob let the blueprint roll itself back up and grabbed two containers of greens out of the fridge along with a bottle of their favorite dressing. A few minutes later he and his housemate were seated at the walnut table in front of the patio doors. He couldn't look out there without seeing Pansy eating his report.

"Dear Lord," prayed Logan. "Thank You for this beautiful day and for terrific neighbors. Thanks for jobs and a place to live and everything You provide for us every day, like this food. I ask that You'd whack Jacob up the side of his head so he'll see the blessings You've put in front of him. In Jesus' name, amen."

Jacob kicked him under the table. "Thanks a lot, man. I see my blessings."

"Do you now?" Logan drizzled dressing over his salad. "How much time have you spent in Eden's backyard? How well do you know Pansy?"

"Would you cut it out already?"

"Ah, so it is a sore spot."

"You're just a big know-it-all and busybody."

"Ooh, pulling out the big guns in the nasty-name contest. Doesn't change the facts, dude. My edjimicated guess is that you're trying to pretend the goat doesn't exist."

Bingo. "Don't be ridiculous."

Logan rolled his eyes. "I'm hearing evasion, not denial. Face up to it."

"The backyard farm is just a passing phase for her. She lost her family and needed something to occupy her." Probably. Hopefully.

"She tell you that?"

Jacob shrugged. "Not in those words, no." He pushed the plate of pasta away. Suddenly not so hungry.

"You're deluding yourself." Logan's voice was quiet. "I think you need to admit there's an eleph — I mean goat in the room, and her name is Pansy."

Eden opened the door at Hailey's knock. "Oh, good, you brought cinnamon rolls."

"Yes, I'm fully aware I owe you four more."

"That would be thirty-four more." Eden stepped back into the living room, allowing her friend room to enter.

"The deal was for one a day for a month. Which stretched out some because the bakery is closed Sundays."

"And then you embarrassed me so badly we agreed on an extra thirty."

"Puh-leeze. I never promised. Besides, you should be thanking me. I got nothing out of the deal except a monetary loss, and you got a steady supply of carbs and a boyfriend."

There was that.

"You just don't want the cinnamon roll train to end." Hailey set the paper bag on the table.

Eden grinned and peeked inside, and the aroma of sweet cinnamon tingled her nostrils. "Nobody makes them like you do." For many women it was chocolate. For her? Cinnamon. Hands down. "Want a coffee before we get started?"

Hailey set her hands on her hips and angled a look at Eden. "It depends. If it's because you're putting off the work, then no. Let's get going and take a break in an hour or two."

Eden couldn't help stroking the bag as she set it on the counter. "Don't even think about it, Licorice." The black cat opened one eye from his spot on the windowsill.

"He looks pretty innocent to me."

"He's such a good boy, aren't you?" Eden cooed as she smoothed the fur on his back.

"I brought bags and boxes. Help me carry them in."

"You're so bossy."

Hailey gave her a searching look. "Have you changed your mind? Do I need to get the girls over to stage an intervention?"

"No." Eden let out a long sigh. "You're right. It's time, even though I'll never be ready. So long as you understand that."

"If you're sure. I've got Rebekah and Kass and Jasmine on one-tap dialing. They'll come."

"Didn't you leave Kass in charge at the bakery?" She followed Hailey out the door and propped it open with a brick before noticing the vehicle in her driveway. "You borrowed Wade's truck?"

"Yeah, he said he'd give me a hand offloading later. I thought it would be better if we removed things from the premises that we've decided you don't need. Wade's up for that."

"But what if I change my mind?"

Hailey tossed flattened boxes out of the pickup bed. "It'll be okay, Eden. Rebekah agrees with me. She was some kind of psych major, remember? She knows these things."

"You've been talking to Rebekah and Wade about me."

"Only because we care about you. Grab an armload of those boxes and take them upstairs. I'll bring the rest and my tape dispenser."

Eden slid the cardboard into a manageable stack and gathered as many as she could. She carried them up the stairs and hesitated. Could she really do this?

"Into the master bedroom," said Hailey from behind her. "Isn't that where we decided to start?"

"Yeah." Eden dumped her load beside the queen bed, still sporting the pink floral spread her mother had loved so much. Loved that it matched the wallpaper.

"So, did you decide about the bed? Are you going to use it?"

Eden glared at Hailey. "Sleep in my parents' bed? Are you kidding me?"

A grin poked Hailey's cheeks upward. "Point taken. Although you'll probably want a queen in here soon enough, so it might make more sense to keep this one than to take it to Salvation Army and then get a different one later."

"I'll cross that bridge when I get to it." If that ever happened. She couldn't imagine Jacob moving into this house any more than she could imagine moving out. Hmm. That didn't bode well.

"Alrighty then." Hailey flipped back the bedspread and began folding it.

Panic enveloped Eden. "What are you doing?"

"Sweetie. You're not keeping the bed. You don't need what's on it. And you hate dusty pink."

Eden swallowed hard and touched her tattoo. "You're right."

Hailey watched her for a moment then folded the rest of the bedding and stacked it in one of the boxes. "Give me a hand getting the mattress and box spring down the stairs."

"Okay."

A few minutes later Hailey swept the closet doors open. "Good space in here. I don't imagine you need any of your mom's clothing. Not your size, not your style. Am I right?"

The lump in Eden's throat would not go away. She nodded.

"You go through the dresser. Here's your box. Everything goes in it, Eden. Everything, unless it's a bona fide keepsake."

She pulled open the bottom drawer. Who would want used men's skivvies and half-worn-out socks? "I think this calls for a garbage bag."

"Good girl. You're right." Hailey tossed one at her. "Do you like the furniture in here? Family heirlooms or something?"

Eden blinked past the tears. "No. I remember the day they brought it home from the department store. It's just cheap pressboard, but they were so excited to have a matching set. The headboard." She swallowed hard. "Two nightstands. The big dresser with the mirror."

"You could get a few antique pieces to put in here. Refinish them. I can help you. Sound like fun?"

"I don't know. Maybe." The bottom drawer empty, Eden shoved it shut and opened the next one. Her mother's nighties and underwear came into view. The tears she'd been blinking back overflowed. "I can't do this, Hailey. I just can't."

Chapter 12

"HEY, JAKEY! HOW DO WE find your house?" His sister's voice came through on the phone. "West Main appears to be a one-way street. Going the wrong direction, I might add."

"Chels! You're in town?" Had she warned him she was coming? Jacob rubbed his hands over his eyes.

"Sierra and I and the kids. We hadn't seen you in a while and decided to spring a visit on you. Plus, we had some errands to run. I hope you're not busy."

Not so much. Eden had turned down his offer for a hike today, saying she had something planned with Hailey. Now there was a pickup truck outside and the girls were hauling furniture out to it. Why hadn't she asked him for help? This was something they could've done together. Not that he wanted to spend a day with Hailey, but still.

"Uh, no. I'm home. Where are you at? Isn't there GPS in that van of Sierra's? Pretty sure it can find my house without any trouble."

Chelsea chuckled. "We have GPS. I wanted to give you a heads-up we were on our way to make sure you were home."

"Come on down." Jacob clicked the phone off and looked the house over. He'd run the vacuum this morning, and it was immaculate. No way his sisters could find any fault with his housekeeping. He looked out the front window as Eden and Hailey struggled to lift a huge dresser into the back of the truck.

That did it. He strapped on his sandals and strode out. "Need a hand?"

"Hey, Jacob." Hailey wiped the back of her hand across her forehead. "This thing is a beast."

"Looks like. Here, let me lift this end and you two get that end." A moment later he'd pushed the dresser as far forward in the pickup box as it could go. He glanced at Eden. Her face was red and puffy like she'd been crying. He hopped down and reached for her. "You okay? What's going on?"

She leaned against him and sniffled. "It's hard."

He looked over her head at Hailey with his eyebrows raised.

"We're cleaning out things that belonged to her parents and sisters." Hailey's jaw jutted out and her eyebrows challenged his.

Why was Hailey helping her, not him? Why hadn't Eden even said anything about needing to do the job? She'd said it was five years since the accident. How was he supposed to guess she'd kept everything this long?

Not that he'd asked how she felt about it. Every time her family came up, she touched that tattoo. He didn't want to add grief to sorrow. Reality smacked him. He hadn't been trying to get to know the complete Eden. Just the one that matched his vision. Logan was right. He needed to do better if they had any hope of a future. And he wanted a future with Eden, right? He pressed a kiss to the top of her head. "Anything else I can help with?"

A vehicle horn tapped twice and an engine cut out. Jacob closed his eyes. Uh oh. He released Eden and looked over at his driveway, where Sierra's van was now parked.

Chelsea bounced out of the passenger side and straight past the rosebushes toward him. "Jakey!"

He gave her a hug, knowing full well what was coming next.

Chelsea's eyes widened. "Eden Andrusek? Is that really you?"

Oh, man. He'd completely forgotten Eden had met his sisters.

"Hi, Chelsea. Yep, it's me."

Might as well own up to everything. It wasn't remotely possible his sisters had missed seeing him holding Eden a minute ago. He twined his fingers through Eden's, tugged her closer, and opened his mouth to announce their relationship.

He hadn't counted on Chelsea. She squealed, grabbed Eden out of his grasp, and did a little dance-and-twirl. "Oh, you two are bad for keeping this a secret."

What could he say? He strode over to the van where his other sister was undoing car seat buckles. "Hey, Sierra."

She straightened and grinned. "Hiya, Jake. I see you've got news for us. Here, let me hand you a toddler. Who wants to see Uncle Jake?"

"Unco Jay!" squealed the little blonde nearest him.

"I'll get her." He lifted Sophie out of her seat. "How's my best girl?"

The two-year-old squished his neck so tightly he could barely breathe.

"Want to give me another one? I have two arms, after all."

Sierra laughed. "Sure. Braden, want to go with Uncle Jake?"

The dark-skinned little boy nodded and climbed over Sophie's seat to reach for Jacob as Sierra got the baby out. Her older daughter triumphantly got her own belt undone and careened toward the door. Jacob crouched and gathered all three kids into a hug. Too many to carry, though. He glanced at his sister, now with the baby on her hip. "I don't know how you do it."

She pressed a kiss to the baby's brown temple. "We're thankful for God's little blessings."

"Sierra! Look what Jakey's been hiding from us!"

Jacob turned to see Chelsea dragging Eden between the rosebushes.

"Remember Eden? She took the animal husbandry course from Keanan and Allison a couple of years ago. You'll never believe it! She's got a goat. You kids want to meet the goat, don't you?"

Braden and Sophie wiggled to get down, so Jacob lowered them to the ground. "Me see goat!" said Sophie, running to Chelsea. Braden stuck his thumb in his mouth and nodded.

Eden glanced back at Hailey. "We can take a little break and visit Pansy. If I'd have known you were coming, I'd have saved the day for you." She looked at Jacob.

He spread his hands and shook his head. "Surprise here, too."

Eden led the way to the side gate. The three kids trooped around her, Chelsea, and Sierra. Jacob elbowed Sierra and took Zoey from her. If he had to spend time in the presence of that menace, he'd hide behind the baby. Call him a chicken, but whatever.

The sight of Jacob holding small children who obviously adored him was nearly Eden's undoing. She barely resisted the impulse to propose to him, then and there, in front of everyone.

Pansy bounded toward her. "Maa."

Hadn't she left the goat in her pen? Apparently not, knowing she'd be home and working with Hailey. Too bad she'd forgotten.

"Goat!" said the little blond girl.

Eden crouched. "Yes, this is Pansy." Good thing the goat was a dwarf breed. She was less likely to send the kids flying.

"Eden, this is Sophie." Sierra knelt beside them. "You might remember hearing we were expecting her when you were a student at Green Acres."

"You'd just met her birth mom and made the arrangements, right?"

Sierra nodded. "Not long after she was born, God sent us Lilly and Braden. They're siblings."

Sophie and Braden were close to the same size. Eden toggled her finger between them. "What's the age difference?"

"Three months." Sierra laughed. "Trust me. It was a zoo when they were babies."

"I bet." Eden glanced at Jacob swinging a squealing baby around. Man, that looked good on him. "What about her?"

"Zoey was unexpected. We couldn't say no when Lilly and Braden's birth mother needed a home for one more." She shook her head. "She's had a tubal ligation now, though. I think our family is complete."

"There chicken!" called Sophie from over by the coop. "Make egg?"

"They sure do. Do you like eggs?"

"Yummy."

Lilly knelt by Pansy and hugged the goat. "I like goats better," she whispered.

Eden grinned at the little girl. She must be about four. "I like goats, too. I like their tasty milk and delicious cheese."

In the background, Jacob stopped swinging the baby.

Zoey? Eden couldn't keep track of all their names. She turned to Chelsea, who was helping Braden rub Pansy's head. "I'm going to start experimenting with goat milk soap this fall."

"Oh, let me know how it goes. I want to do that someday, too, but everything on the farm is so busy between the school and all the kids." She sat back on her heels and looked over at Jacob. "I wanted you to know that Keanan and I are expecting, too."

Jacob grinned at his sister. "Really? Congrats."

"I'm surprised this lot didn't scare her off," Sierra said.

"On the contrary, I'd never had much to do with babies before this lot, as you put it. So now I'm a total expert in changing cloth diapers and shushing cranky infants. And mixing formula, but hopefully that's a skill I won't need to exercise."

"When are you due?" Eden asked.

"February. Keanan is over-the-moon excited."

Eden snuck a glance at Jacob, but he'd turned away, his face hidden behind the baby's curly black hair. Would these be her sisters-in-law, her nieces, her nephew one day? Would Jacob thrill to the idea of being a father? Surely he would. She had only to look at him with these little ones to see it already, except maybe for baby spit-up. And would he be a diaper-changing daddy? Surely the other kind didn't exist in this day and age, but it was hard to imagine him willingly getting his hands dirty.

Maybe it was a good thing they were taking it slow. Was it because they were each looking for reasons to bail out, or was slow a good thing? Back up a step. Was she looking for a reason to break up with him? Surely not. She loved him.

Then why hadn't she confided in him how hard it was to get rid of her parents' stuff? Her sisters' things, like the gown Indigo had bought for prom but never had the chance to wear? Jacob hadn't asked. But she also hadn't told him.

She surged to her feet. "Why don't I go inside and fix a pitcher of iced tea? I'm sure you all must be thirsty after your long drive."

"Sounds great." Chelsea straightened. "Let me give you a hand."

Jacob offered the baby to Chelsea. "I've got it." He snagged Eden's hand as they walked toward the back steps.

She leaned against him, aware of watching eyes but not caring. The screen door banged shut behind them, and she turned to face him in the dimly-lit kitchen. "Your sisters are great."

"You are what's great." Jacob tugged her close and covered her mouth with his.

Eden melted against him. He'd felt the same way she did, watching the little ones. Everything was going to work out. She'd be more open, sharing her memories. About her plans for her backyard farm and Pansy. He'd learn to accept the goat and relax a bit more. They were good together. Good for each other.

Someone cleared a throat. "I heard we were making a pitcher of iced tea?"

Eden pulled away from Jacob and whirled to face Hailey standing in the dining room. "Um, yes. A pitcher of iced tea. I'm making one. For the children."

"Do you want Wade and me to take what we've already loaded and deal with it? We can finish the rest another day."

"I-I don't know." Eden glanced at Jacob.

"I don't imagine they'll stay long," he said. "Maybe an hour. You don't need to change your plans for them. I can get them out of your hair then come give a hand when they're gone. If you want me to."

Eden opened a cupboard and pulled out a glass pitcher. "That works." He wanted to help. They'd get through this weird spot. They would.

Hailey swung her purse. "I'll call Wade then. Be back in about an hour with an empty truck."

Eden froze. What had they already loaded? Was she really ready to say goodbye to all her parents' things? She let out a long breath. "Okay. Thanks."

"No prob." Hailey's voice took on a more teasing note. "Behave yourself."

As if that even deserved a reply.

Chapter 13

IT DIDN'T SEEM LIKE HIS sisters had come to visit him at all. They sat on Eden's back porch drinking iced tea and visiting while the children bounded around with the goat. Except Zoey, of course. Jacob had snagged the baby, more from a need for something to focus on than to do Sierra a favor. He replied to Zoey's babble with nonsense words of his own, and she giggled, patting his face.

He hadn't even come into Eden's backyard since the day he'd fixed the fence over a month ago. Now, sitting on an ancient wooden deck chair listening to the three women chatter about the best goat cheese recipes and where to get organic chicken feed, he knew he'd been deluding himself. Logan was right. There weren't any signs that the stupid goat was a phase Eden was nearly done with.

God? Jacob hoped the Almighty didn't mind that he blew a raspberry on the baby's neck while praying. *I'm kinda confused here. You know I don't want to be a farmer. It's why I turned down the offer from Green Acres. That, and I really believed You were calling me to work with Global Sunbeams, but I'll admit it. I'm not that fond of animals or... muck.*

Muck. How clean was the yard? His eyes sprang open. Were the kids going to be covered in goat manure? The ground looked okay. The air didn't smell ripe. It might be okay. Anyway, that was Sierra's problem.

God, why did You make me love a woman with a goat?

It wasn't precisely God's fault. God hadn't been the one to ask Eden out that first time. That'd been all Jacob.

The women stood and hugged each other.

Jacob blinked. He'd missed a cue.

"It was so good to see you again," Chelsea gushed at Eden before glancing at Jacob. "And so bad of my brother to keep you a secret. You guys should come up for a weekend sometime." She looked over at the goat cavorting with the three children. "Although I guess she ties you down some."

Understatement.

Eden glanced at him. "Maybe sometime. We'll see. I do have friends who can help out with Pansy at times."

She'd never mentioned it to him. Was he not worth her while to get a goat-sitter occasionally?

Chelsea and Eden rounded up the older three, who didn't want to leave their new friend, while Sierra reached for Zoey. "You found one of the good ones," his sister whispered.

He knew it, but the conflict inside him didn't just float away on a fluffy cloud. He quirked a grin. "She's pretty awesome."

"Who'd have thought you'd fall for an urbanite with a backyard farm? God has a sense of humor."

Sierra knew him too well. He couldn't even claim to have fallen in love before knowing about Pansy. No, he'd met the goat first. He shrugged. "It is kind of strange. I'm not sure how it happened."

The gate closed behind the others, leaving him and Sierra

in privacy.

His sister laughed. “There’s no accounting for love. Just know it’s worth the work, Jake. The give and take is like a dance. Two steps forward, two steps back, but when you’re in each other’s arms and in tune, it’s effortless.”

Jacob crossed his arms. “I’m not sure what you’re saying.”

“I see the expression on your face when you look at Pansy. If you and Eden haven’t argued about it yet, I bet it’s coming. That goat means a lot to her.”

“You mentioned two steps forward and two steps back. Maybe the goat is her two steps back.”

Sierra’s eyebrows rose. “I think you’re saying if she loves you enough, she’d get rid of Pansy.”

Well, duh. He stared at his sister.

“Oh, boy. You want her to change an intrinsic part of who she is. A very important part, I might add, and a part I totally agree with.”

“Women always side together.”

“No, Jacob. We don’t. You need to take a long hard look at your attitude, because what you’re feeling isn’t love. Love is patient and kind. It wants the best for the other person. Love gives lavishly to the other person. Nothing matters but his or her happiness.”

Jacob took a deep breath. It was difficult holding Sierra’s gaze while her words crashed into his soul. It would do no good to remind her it went both ways. She was right, but that didn’t mean anything had changed. “Thanks for caring,” he said stiffly.

“Oh, Jake. You’re my little brother. I can’t help caring.” Sierra gave him a hug, the baby giggling as she nestled between them. “I’m glad we came today. It was spur-of-the-moment, but I can see God's hand all over it. We'll be praying for you. I love you, buddy."

Zoey blew kisses as Sierra carried her out of the backyard.

Jacob stared at the goat, who'd skittered over to her water bowl.

A moment later, doors slammed and a motor started then faded away. The gate latch rattled as Eden came back through it.

"Maa." Pansy crow-hopped toward Eden, who bent to rub the small goat's head. She murmured something Jacob couldn't quite catch then glanced up and saw him still sitting on the back porch.

He forced a smile. "Sorry for the invasion."

"Don't be. I needed the break. But I guess Hailey will be back anytime, and we have a lot more stuff to go through." Eden crossed the back porch and reached for the screen door handle.

Jacob followed her into the kitchen. "I think we need to talk."

She eyed him warily and bit her lip. "I'm not sure I like the sounds of that. Did I embarrass you in front of your family? I'm sorry."

"No, it's not that." He forced a chuckle. "My sisters adore you. Did you miss the thumbs-up they gave me? Maybe that was behind your back."

Eden touched her tattoo then crossed her arms. "Well, that's good. Then what is it?"

"Hallooo! Anyone home?" called Hailey from the front door. "Are we ready to get back to work?"

Jacob came to a quick decision. "Can I help you girls with your project? We can talk later."

Eden searched his face. "If you really want to, I won't turn you down. There will be a lot of boxes to carry down to the truck."

He flexed his muscles. "Then I'm your man." He only hoped that was really true.

It was late afternoon before Hailey drove away in Wade's truck for the last time. Guilt overwhelming her, Eden paused in the doorway of the master bedroom. How could she have gotten rid of all those things? Just deleted the memories as though Indigo, Anya, and their parents had never existed?

Jacob's arms encircled her from behind, and she leaned back against him, closing her eyes. "You did well," he said quietly.

"I feel like a traitor." She resisted the impulse to rub the roses.

"You're not one. Not at all." His words soothed, just a little.

"It's so empty. I don't know what to do next."

"Peel off the wallpaper? Put in new flooring?"

"Maybe." Mom had loved that huge floral print on the walls. "The carpets are bad, aren't they?" It wasn't even a question. They were older than she was, matted and stained. He was right. They needed to go, but how could she afford to replace them?

Jacob released her and crouched in the doorway. "I wonder what's under them. Mind if I check?"

Why hadn't she ever been curious? She wrapped her arms around her waist, chilled with his touch gone. "Go for it."

"The tack strip here is down tightly. That's good." He moved over to the window and pried up a heat register then loosened the carpet and peeked underneath. "You might be in luck."

"What do you mean?" Eden knelt beside him. "What am I looking at?"

"Hardwood, I think. From the little I can see, it might be oak."

A tingle of excitement ran through her. "Can what's under there be worse than the carpet?"

Jacob grinned at her. "I don't see how."

"Then let's find out."

He pulled a folding knife from his pocket. "Once I start cutting, there's no going back."

Eden nodded then held her breath as he sliced into the matted gray carpet then the dense underlay, careful not to gouge the wood beneath. A few minutes later he turned back a corner to expose more than a square foot of golden oak. She ran her fingers over the smooth surface. "Why would they cover that up?"

"Who knows why people do what they do?" Jacob glanced at her. "Wall-to-wall carpet is softer, warmer."

"I guess." Visions of polished floors danced through her mind. "Let's rip it up. This room first."

"I'll go get my tools." Jacob's eyes twinkled as he kissed her cheek. "Unless you've replaced your princess set with real ones."

She smacked his arm lightly. "Hey, they work for me."

He chuckled and stood. "Like I said. I'll be back in a couple of minutes."

Eden leaned against the wall, knees tucked up to her chin, and listened to his footsteps disappear down the stairs. The front door squeaked open and closed. The part of her that felt disloyalty to her family was losing the battle in the light of current possibilities. She looked at the tattoo as she traced the roses' outline with a fingertip. "Mom? Dad? Anya? Indigo? I will always miss you, but I'm alive, and you're... not." Her throat didn't choke the way it usually did when she thought of moving on. Five years was enough.

She looked around the space. For once she was doing something right. The wallpaper had to come off. Soak it? Scrape it? What color would she paint? Maybe a fresh aqua against white trim.

Not that blue with a greenish tinge went with her bedding.

Wait, was she really considering moving into this room? But why not? It was no longer a shrine to her parents. She didn't need to sleep in the tiniest room. She'd get herself new bedding while she was at it. Put white curtains at the window. In her mind's eye, she could see them billowing in the summer breeze.

Would Jacob like aqua? Would he one day share this room with her? Maybe she shouldn't have gotten rid of the queen after all. Oh, man. Memories of her parents' penchant for Sunday afternoon naps taunted her. As she'd grown older, she'd realized the muffled sounds seeping out from beneath the closed door were not snoring.

Yes. She'd been right to get rid of their bed. Definitely.

The front door opened downstairs. Jacob whistled as he jogged up the stairs. He set down a shiny red toolbox just inside the bedroom door then straightened and met her gaze.

Eden stood and strolled over, drinking in the sight of him. She stretched out both arms, and he pulled her close as his gaze locked on hers.

"Thanks, Jacob." She tipped her face upward.

He dropped a quick kiss to her mouth. "For what?"

"For being here. For caring about me."

"It's my pleasure." His hands slid up her back and caught in her ponytail. He tugged the elastic free and slid his fingers through her hair while thumbs caressed her cheeks. The intensity in his gaze strengthened. "I love you."

Jacob didn't leave time for her response. He captured her mouth with his and gave her a solid demonstration.

She didn't need words to reply, anyway.

Chapter 14

JACOB SAT IN HIS BOSS'S OFFICE and rubbed his forehead. "I'd really rather not."

Dean's eyebrows rose. "I thought you'd be chomping at the bit. You're usually happy to pack a bag and head anywhere in the world at a moment's notice."

That was before he'd met Eden. How could he handle a month away from her at this crucial stage of their relationship?

"I had Ian scheduled to go, but there are complications with his wife's pregnancy. He's needed here."

"I can see that." Would Eden's belly someday be round with his child? He snapped his mind back to his boss. "No one else can cover?"

Dean steepled his fingers. "No one with enough experience. I'd push off the trip, but everything is in place there already. The container with the panels arrived in port last week and has cleared customs. A truck driver who can translate has been hired. Villages are waiting."

"When would I need to leave?" Jacob couldn't say no. Man, he wished he could.

"Wednesday afternoon. You'll fly Seattle-New York-Dubai-Nampula."

Jacob pressed his temples. "What about Bridgeview Community Center? I was going to start that installation next week." Was going to. Yeah, he was giving in. He could feel it.

"I'll send Ian." Dean chuckled. "It's only fair he does your work."

"No." The word was out before Jacob had time to think about it. "It's my neighborhood. I want to be the one to do it. They'll be okay with waiting." He hoped.

"I didn't realize you were that settled into Spokane."

Jacob shrugged. "I like it here."

"There must be a woman involved."

He hadn't planned to explain Eden to Dean any time soon. Jacob nodded.

"I'm sorry, man. If I had anyone else to send, I'd do it. But I really need you on the ground in Mozambique. Will you go?"

What would happen if he said no? Would his boss fire him? But Dean knew he'd go. Jacob had spent his entire life making sure he met expectations. It wasn't a habit he could overthrow lightly.

He sighed heavily. "I guess so. You leave me no choice."

Dean's eyes warmed in sympathy as he slid a packet across the desk to Jacob. "This has your flight info and everything else you need to know. Go through it and ask me any questions before Wednesday. Of course, you can call my direct line anytime."

Jacob nodded and picked up the paperwork.

"Take the next couple of days off to prepare for the trip. And take that girl of yours out for dinner to make up for leaving her." Dean fumbled in a desk drawer and came out with a small card. "A gift certificate to the Wild Sage Bistro. Here you go."

Jacob tried a grin. "Thanks." He stopped by his cubicle to shut down his computer and file the plans he'd been working on. Somebody else would finish those. Maybe Ian.

Eden studied Jacob across the table at the Wild Sage. He'd sounded nervous when he called to invite her to dinner. He'd been rather quiet since he opened his car door for her, and his kiss had been short and... dutiful? He wouldn't bring her to an expensive place like this just to break up with her, would he? But the other alternative was a proposal, and that didn't make sense, either.

Jacob did everything thoroughly. A guy like him wouldn't pop the question without thinking things through and making sure she was ready. She'd be lucky to hear those words from him on Christmas Eve, or even Valentine's Day. He'd never do it after only five weeks of dating.

The waiter set two glasses of pomegranate ginger spritzer on the polished wood table. Eden usually ordered water, but Jacob had pointed out the booze-free section of the drinks menu and invited her to try something new. This didn't seem the Jacob she knew. They'd caught plenty of weekend lunches out, but nothing close to the atmosphere and prices here. Yet he'd insisted she choose an appetizer and dessert as well as an entree.

If he were going to end their relationship, he was certainly doing it in style. He'd better have the conversation at the end of the meal, because she wouldn't be able to eat afterward, and this was an experience to be absorbed and cherished.

Jacob reached across the table and captured her hands. She couldn't read the expression on his face, but that was nothing new. He rubbed a thumb over her palm.

Eden couldn't stand it anymore. "What's the big occasion?" She tried to keep her voice light. 'This is pretty upscale for an impromptu Monday-night date. I might've had other plans." He knew her life well enough to doubt that. At least besides milking.

A small smile tugged at his lips.

That was better. Maybe she could breathe again.

Jacob studied her. "How was work today?"

Seriously? She gave a slight shrug. "Nothing unusual. A puppy loose in one of the parks." She turned the tables. "How about you?"

His gaze lingered on her face for a few seconds then at their joined hands.

Panic returned. "You didn't lose your job, did you? Or get transferred out of Spokane?"

"No. I'm being sent on assignment."

Eden dared breathe. "And what does that mean, exactly?"

"It means I'm leaving on Wednesday for Mozambique." He met her gaze. "For a month."

"Oh. You had me worried for a minute there."

His forehead furrowed. "What do you mean?"

"I figured you must have brought me here to break up with me, though it seemed excessive."

He pulled back a little. "You thought what?"

It did seem silly now. "I can't read you, Jacob. You're so pre-occupied that I was sure I'd done something wrong. Said something to put you off."

"Never. I'm sorry to have caused worry." His grin went sideways. "This is a little different for me, isn't it? I'll be honest. My boss gave me a gift certificate. Told me to take out my best girl and make a memory before I left."

So the Wild Sage Bistro hadn't been his idea. Eden wasn't sure what to think about that. Nothing. It was innocent. Would she have wanted him to turn it down? Not when the crab wonton appetizers that had stealthily appeared on their table were so amazing.

"That was nice of him. So tell me about your trip. What will you be doing?"

"A container-load of solar panels and batteries arrived in port there last week and have cleared customs. Now they all need to be distributed and installed."

"So this has been planned for a long time?" He could've bothered to mention it.

"Ian was supposed to go. It's early enough in his wife's pregnancy that it should have been fine, but they've had some complications. None of the other guys has the experience to simply step in. Just me."

Sounded legit. There went her plans for the summer. All the hikes and picnics she'd dreamed of. Stripping wallpaper and painting walls with him. To say nothing of kisses in the moonlight. "A whole month?"

"Thirty-three days. Not that anyone counted them." He offered a rueful grin.

"That's such a long time." Almost as long as they'd already known each other.

"It will seem forever."

"Not for you. You'll be doing something different every single day. Meeting new people, having new adventures. I'll be doing the same-old."

"I'll miss you every single day. Every hour. I tried to talk Dean out of sending me. I don't want to leave you."

"Does this happen often?"

"What, the international trips? Dean usually sets up two or three a year."

"And how often do you go?"

"I've been to Africa half a dozen times, maybe? The first was with Chelsea's husband, Keanan. He introduced me to the opportunities for solar in developing countries while I was in college." He leaned over the table, his eyes alight. "The need is so great. Without solar, they have no light after sundown. They have to pump water from their wells by hand or, if they're not lucky enough to have a village well, carry jars of water on their heads from the river. They have to gather sticks and dung for cook fires and tend them constantly. Grains must be pounded with mortar and pestle. Solar changes everything, and it's renewable, sustainable, and nonintrusive."

She hadn't heard so much passion in Jacob's voice before, or such a long speech, either. This truly was what he lived for, not a job he'd landed simply because it was open.

"What about the community complex?" She'd heard something akin to that intensity in his voice the night of his presentation, too. "Isn't that on the schedule for the end of July?"

Jacob grimaced. "I stopped by to talk to Ray Santoro today and asked if it could be postponed until I returned. I really want to do that install myself."

So other people in Bridgeview had known before she did. That felt... awkward. But had she really wanted to be told by text? No. "What did he say?"

"He has to run it by the board, but doesn't think it will be a problem. My boss said he could send someone else to do it if needed."

"But it's your project."

"Technically it is Global Sunbeams' project. Anyway, I can't do anything about it. Either the board will let it wait, or Dean will make sure it gets done."

The waiter hovered at the end of the table. "May I bring your main course?"

Eden stared at the plate between them. Somehow they'd each nibbled a few of the crab wontons. She scooped the last one. "Yes, thank you." The food was so delicious she really ought to pay more attention to it. It was costing Jacob's boss a small fortune.

A moment later, the delectable aromas of wild mushrooms, goat cheese, and chicken reached her. Jacob's plate looked equally incredible, loaded with pork tenderloins and fettuccini. "This smells amazing." She took a small bite, and the flavors melted in her mouth. "Oh, wow. I could kiss your boss."

Jacob quirked a grin sideways. "I should have thought of coming here myself." His eyes met hers.

"I could kiss you anyway," she whispered.

"I'd let you." His gaze searched hers. "I might even kiss you back."

Eden set her fork down. "A whole month apart?"

"I know. Let's talk about other things for now, so we can enjoy this meal. There will be time to say goodbye tomorrow."

Eden pushed a morsel of chicken into the purple mashed potatoes. She could do this. Who knew if she'd ever dine at the Wild Sage again? Would Jacob still want her when he came back from gallivanting around the world, or would he meet someone else? Someone without a goat?

Jacob held Eden in his arms in the moonlight on Tuesday evening. They'd wandered down along the river's edge among the trees. A distant coyote yipped, and a few dogs barked in reply. A fresh breeze caressed his cheeks.

"I'm going to miss you," he whispered against her lips before kissing her again.

"Email me every day. Please."

"I won't always have access to the Internet, but I will as often as I can. It will go quickly. I'll be back before you know it." He wished he believed that himself, but she'd been right. It was likely to drag out more for her than for him. He'd be immersed in new experiences, and she'd be at home with all their shared memories as well as her regular duties.

"You won't forget me?"

"Never, Eden." He pressed her tighter against him and kissed her thoroughly. He could never forget this woman whom God had made for him, who fit him so completely. Thoughts like that could get him in trouble. Maybe it was a good thing he was heading for the other side of the world. It would give both of them time to cool, time to think. That would be good, right? It had to be good, because it was happening, and he was powerless to stop it.

Chapter 15

"HEARD FROM JACOB LATELY?" Hailey peeled a huge swath of wallpaper off the master bedroom wall.

Eden needed to stop thinking of it as her parents' refuge. It was going to be hers when it was all finished. "Twice. Once when he got there and again the next day when he said they were leaving on a trip to some remote villages."

Hailey planted her hands on her hips. "Only two times? He's been gone five days."

"I know." Eden picked at a stubborn bit of paper. "But I can't make rural Africa have Internet, can I?"

"I guess not. Are you worried about him?"

"What's with the twenty questions?"

"You are worried."

"Am not. He's perfectly safe."

"You're worried about your relationship."

Eden stared her friend down. "You are reading far too much into this and putting words in my mouth besides."

Hailey's eyebrows shot up. "I've known you forever, girl. You can't hide your emotions from me."

She could try. Hailey's words were more on target than

Eden cared to admit. "You know what? I think a bit of time apart will be good for us. We'll have a chance to evaluate and see if we've got what it takes to go the distance. You might think that's a negative, but I don't."

Hailey shook her head. "If he jumped at the chance to go to Africa for that reason, you guys are in serious trouble."

"He did not jump at the chance to go. He has a job. He was sent because he has the qualifications. He has a double degree in architecture and engineering, and he's been to Africa six times before. His boss doesn't need to worry about him getting the task done correctly."

"I still think something is rotten in Denmark."

Thanks for nothing, Hailey. "If you're going to be such a raincloud, why don't you just go home? I'll get the paper stripped myself." Sooner or later.

"I told you I'd help, and I'm here."

"Then stop trash-talking Jacob. I'm a big girl, and I can handle this."

Hailey shrugged and moved to a new section of the wall.

Eden glared at her back. "What's your problem anyway? PMS?"

"Not everything can be attributed to hormones, Eden. Thanks."

"Well, something has you riled, and you're taking it out on me. So tell me already. Maybe I can help." Hopefully she could actually be more help than Hailey had been, planting doubts in her head about Jacob. She didn't need help. She was perfectly capable of messing up her relationships all by herself. Look at the mess she was making just talking to Hailey.

"You know I thought maybe I'd have a chance with Logan."

Eden bit her tongue so hard she tasted blood. Hailey hadn't stopped throwing herself at Jacob's housemate since the middle of June. When would she figure out he wasn't interested? "What happened?"

Hailey sighed dramatically. "Jasmine and Linnea came into the bakery yesterday, and I overheard them talking about him."

Eden stepped back. The entire window wall was now free of giant flowers. She turned to the angled side wall. "What did they say?" Not that she was into gossip, but Hailey needed a listening ear to get this out of her system.

"He asked Linnea out to a ball game."

"Interesting." Looked like this corner of wallpaper was a little loose.

"Eden Andrusek! You're not even listening. He asked Linnea on a date."

"Yes?" Eden turned to see her friend's glare.

"Why didn't he ask me? I love baseball."

"Since when? I don't think you've been to five games since high school."

Hailey grimaced. "I still like it, though. And I'd have been delighted to go with him."

"You are trying way too hard. I don't think you'd be happy with Logan anyway. He's not really your type."

"He sure can play that piano." Hailey sighed.

A vision of Lucy and Schroeder from the Peanuts cartoon popped into Eden's head, and she couldn't quite choke back the chuckle.

"What's so funny about that?"

"Nothing. You're right. He's very talented. Hailey, listen to me."

Hailey dropped her chin and narrowed her gaze. "What?"

"When Mr. Right comes, it will be mutual, and you'll know it."

"One month of dating, and now you're an expert?"

"You know it's true. I was right about this before I met Jacob."

"Uh huh." Hailey pushed aside a pile of damp wallpaper with her foot. "So you and Jacob are going to get married and live happily ever after?"

This deserved an honest answer. "I don't know for sure yet. But we have a good foundation."

"I'm not certain you do. I don't think he's touched Pansy yet. That goat means everything to you. And then there's the chickens. Has he told you what he thinks of your backyard farm?"

Hailey's words pierced through Eden's armor to her heart. "I'm sure it will be fine." He loved her, didn't he? He said so. He kissed her like he meant it, while treating her with respect. What more could she want?

She could want a guy who liked her goat.

"You're living in denial, girl. He wants nothing to do with your menagerie. If he hasn't asked you to give it up for him, that discussion is coming. He's not going to change, but he'll ask you to."

"You're wrong." Even to herself, Eden's voice sounded weak.

"Keep telling yourself that. Maybe you'll be lucky."

Eden turned her back on Hailey and pulled at the next piece of wallpaper. Grr. Why couldn't her best friend keep her opinions to herself? Weren't friends supposed to be supportive?

Silence stretched along with the shadows as time went on.

Could Hailey be right? Were she and Jacob in trouble, and

she'd been avoiding confronting the elephant in the room? More like the goat.

Time for a complete change of subject. "How are things at the bakery these days?" Probably Hailey was glaring at her back now, but Eden didn't turn around to see.

"Good. Kass is experimenting with chilled soups for summer, and our clientele is lapping them up."

"Sounds like a good idea. It's been so hot lately. I've been eating a lot of salad. Just can't be bothered cooking."

"You should feel the temperature in the kitchen, even with the exhaust fans running. It's brutal in there. We have spot fans on every available surface."

Eden couldn't even imagine. "I guess there's more than one reason I'm not a chef."

"It's not for the faint of heart, that's for sure. We're lucky we're on the south side of the street. At least the customers catch a break."

"You should talk to Jacob when he gets back. He might have some ideas on how to beat the heat in that kitchen."

Silence.

Argh, she'd done it to herself, bringing Jacob back into the conversation. But he was an important part of her life, so it was natural his name would crop up sometimes, right?

"We had consultants go over everything before we renovated." Hailey's voice had chilled. "No matter how many degrees he has in what, he doesn't know more than the guys from the state health and building code departments."

"I didn't mean—"

"Forget it, Eden."

"Hailey, I didn't mean you and Kass hadn't done your homework. I know you did. You're thorough in everything you do."

"Thank you."

They were down to one wall still covered with gigantic flowers. Surely they could find something to talk about for a few minutes that had nothing to do with men. They'd been friends most of their lives. It shouldn't be this hard.

But it was.

Last time Jacob had been in Africa, it had been the dead of winter in the States, and the midst of a hot, humid summer in Mozambique. This time around, the relative coolness of an African winter was welcome after several weeks of ninety-degree-plus days back home.

Back home. Was he thinking of Spokane that way now? Home had always been Portland, but how did that saying go? Home is where the heart is. Eden had claimed his heart, so that made Spokane home.

But had he claimed hers? One glance at her email address when he'd entered it in his phone had made him cringe. Goatinthecity indeed.

This was crazy. Goats had a place, like at the farm his sisters shared with their friends in Idaho. If he wanted a goat, he'd have moved to Green Acres. Why had he fallen in love with someone who thought livestock belonged in an urban area?

A nagging thought bubbled in the back of his mind, but he pushed it away. Of course he loved Eden. But if that were true, why couldn't he accept her lifestyle? He'd gotten over the tattoo of roses once she'd explained the reasoning behind it. He didn't love it, but he could understand it.

There was no understanding Pansy. She couldn't possibly bring in enough income to be worth the expense and hassle of keeping her, though Dad had reminded Jacob a few times that life wasn't all about money.

Of course he knew that. Every time he came to Africa, the huge smiles of people living in poverty challenged him. They were satisfied with so little, but they didn't really know any different. Didn't expect more, so every solar cooker, every solar well pump they could provide was reason enough for a celebration.

The Land Rover lurched to a stop at the next village. Men, women, children, chickens, dogs, and goats surged toward the vehicle in welcome.

Of course goats. There was no escape from them, no matter where he went.

"How about this?" Eden held the pale aqua paint chip up to a cotton blend in the well-lit fabric store.

Adriana fingered the cloth. "For a comforter cover or for the windows? You might find that to have a bit much pattern."

Eden chuckled. "I guess you didn't see what came out. Just call it a riot of roses, nineteen-eighties style. This is downright soothing in comparison."

Her friend shuddered then reached for another bolt. "How about this? The variation is more in the texture than in multiple colors."

"Hmm. It does go nicely with the paint. It reminds me of the deep sea. Are you sure it won't be too, well, boring?"

"You're looking for light and airy. Soothing. Not too feminine, right?" Adriana winked. "If the rumors I've been hearing around the neighborhood are correct."

Eden would ignore that. After two weeks and very few emails, she was no longer certain. "Airy is a good start, for sure. I have this vision of curtains fluttering in the breeze."

"Okay. You'll probably want a room-darkening shade then, with something gauzy overtop. How about this?" Adriana pointed at an open-weave batiste in white. "We can use this one—" she picked up the dark aqua "—for a comforter cover and the roll-up shade, and the batiste for the curtains." She angled her head and narrowed her eyes as she laid the two bolts together. "The batiste would make a great bed skirt, too, tightly gathered. What do you think?"

The picture focused in Eden's mind's eye. "I think that would look nice. The floor is oak, by the way. It's a bit worn in places, but I'll leave it as is for now."

"It must be quite the transformation up there." Adriana studied her. "I can't wait to see what you've done. Is the downstairs next?"

That was one thing about starting. There was no good place to stop. "I might have to save up a bit of money before I tackle the main floor. Once I move into the bigger space, I'll tear apart my current room."

"Only two bedrooms?" Adriana frowned. "You three girls shared one? Must've been crowded."

Eden swallowed hard. "No, Indigo and Anya shared. I had my own." And then an entire house all to herself.

"So what about your sisters' bedroom? Are you doing that one, too?"

"Yes." Eden blinked back tears and fished another paint chip out of her purse to keep her fingers busy. "We emptied it and painted it a pale lavender. It sure beats the lilac clusters in the old wallpaper. Reminded me of Bloomsday."

Adriana chuckled as she took the colored card. "Yes, we Spokanites do love our Lilac Festival, don't we? So what are we doing for that one? Same thing, only in purples?"

"I hadn't thought that far. I'm not sure what I'm putting in the room, to be honest. I got rid of the beds and dressers. They weren't in good shape, and... I just couldn't face looking at them anymore."

"I see." Adriana tapped the aqua paint chip. "Are you putting a queen in this room?"

"I don't know. I was thinking of moving my twin bed into there and just getting new bedding."

"I heard you and Jacob Riehl were getting serious."

"Don't believe every rumor you hear."

"So it's not true?"

"He's been in Africa for two weeks. I've heard from him four times. While I know he's far from the city and very busy, I don't know what to think. And besides..." Eden took a deep breath. "He doesn't like Pansy."

"That's a problem." Adriana studied her. "How much do you love him? Would you give up Pansy for him?"

Eden narrowed her gaze. "Should I have to? Is it fair of him to ask that of me?"

"Has he said anything?"

"No. We just don't talk about her or hang around in my backyard. At first I thought staying away from my house was a good idea, lest we be too tempted to... you know."

Adriana's gaze remained neutral.

"But now that we've been apart for a while, I'm not so sure. Not about the temptation, I mean. But maybe I'm kidding myself about the realities of actually fitting into each other's lives."

"We can't buy fabric until you decide what size of bed we're covering, Eden. That doesn't mean you have to choose today whether you're marrying Jacob or not, but your choice will tell me how serious you are about moving forward at all. Of having that talk with him when he returns."

"Queen or twin. A life with someone or keeping to myself."

Adriana nodded. "Or there's always a king." She released a small smile. "More fun, but I can tell you, it seems really large since Stephan died."

Eden met Adriana's eyes with sympathy. "I don't think I could get a king up that staircase anyway. I'll price out a queen, and see if I can get it into my budget."

"Way to go, girl." Adriana reached out and enveloped Eden in a hug. "You won't regret the investment."

Chapter 16

JESUS WANTS ME FOR A sunbeam," sang a group of African children in their quaint accent.

Jacob grinned. Now that was a children's hymn he hadn't heard in recent years.

The missionary beside him chuckled. "We thought it would be a fitting way to commemorate the installation of the solar panels. We all need reminders that we are to be reflections of God's light to the world around us."

"We do." Jacob did, too.

A moment later the children shifted to Sunshine in My Soul. "There is sunshine in my soul today, more glorious and bright, than glows in any earthly sky, for Jesus is my light."

"I see you went all out with the theme," Jacob whispered. How had he forgotten all the links his solar career had with his Christian faith? What happened when the storm clouds rolled in? That's why solar panels were hooked up to batteries to store the energy. In fact, there was little use in trying to store sunlight for use in the daytime, when it was really needed at night and on overcast days. If he was Jesus' sunbeam, did that only count when life was cheery and happy? Or did his soul have batteries, too, to keep shining even when circumstances were dreary?

He'd known few truly bleak days. Not with loving parents and enough money to smooth the rough patches he'd come across. But still, he'd allowed circumstances to inform his attitude on too many occasions, even with Eden.

"There is gladness in my soul today, and hope and praise and love, for blessings which He gives me now, for joys laid up above."

It was time to truly grow up. To think of others ahead of himself. To look at Eden as a complete person, not just the part of her that attracted him. How could he expect her to change for him if he refused to change for her?

"Jesus is my light." Jacob cradled his lowered head as the final words of the refrain washed over him. Yes, Lord. Let it be so. Let me walk in Your sunshine.

"Time for a sleepover!" Hailey fell back against the fluffy comforter covering Eden's new bed.

Kass fingered the gauzy curtains. "This is gorgeous, Eden. I didn't know you could sew."

"Adriana helped pick the fabric and did all the sewing. I probably owe her free goat milk for life."

"Well, the two of you chose a stunning combination. I like the furniture, too."

Hailey sat upright. "I'd hoped we could hunt down some antiques to restore, but Eden found these on craigslist, already done. Shabby chic might be a bit out of style, but the whitewashed look does go well with the room."

Eden laughed. "I've rarely been accused of being in style."

"Oh, don't be silly. Your wardrobe is très chic." Hailey blew a kiss. "At least the pieces you wear out of the house."

"Hey, I have chores to do. Pansy will wreck Lululemon as quickly as Sally Ann. And who'd wear anything pricey to paint walls?"

"I was giving your other outfits a compliment, girl." Thankfully Hailey's humor had improved.

"When's Jacob back?" asked Kass.

"One more week. I can't believe how quickly the month has flown by."

"Having a big project helped, I'm sure. And you're well on the way in your old bedroom, too. What are you going to use that space for?"

"I really don't know. If I had desperately needed extra room for anything, I might have tackled this job sooner." Eden sat beside Hailey on the bed. "Thanks for pushing me."

"You're welcome. That's what friends do." Hailey leaned against Eden's arm and gave her a significant look. "Don't forget it."

"Goes both ways." Eden nudged Hailey back. "I heard Linnea and Logan talking the other day through the fence. Mingled with the aromas of barbecued steak."

Hailey grimaced. "Don't remind me. I'm over him. The right man for me is out there somewhere. Or maybe he and Linnea will have a disagreement, and he'll notice me again."

"Like he ever did." Kass shook her head, chuckling. "You don't sound like you're over him at all."

"But I am." Hailey tossed a cushion at her cousin. "I'm a business woman, and I speak my mind."

"You sure do." Eden couldn't help laughing. "You

terrified Logan."

Hailey stuck her nose in the air. "The right man will value me for who I am as well as for my charming personality."

Her words pierced Eden. She'd never admit to her girlfriends how nervous she was about Jacob's return and her decision to confront him about his attitude toward Pansy. The hard thing to accept was that he had as much right to prefer goldfish as she did to prefer goats. If she refused to change — or just plain couldn't — what right did she have to expect it of him? None.

"Don't forget your wonderful man will also value you for your deep humility," Kass added.

Hailey smiled smugly. "That too, of course."

"Oh, you two." Eden shoved aside her nerves. "Come on downstairs. I tried a new goat cheese recipe last night, this time with rosemary. Want to try some on crackers?"

"Sounds good." Kass started toward the door.

"Would you really rather have that than cinnamon rolls?" asked Hailey, her voice full of innocence.

Eden pushed her friend backward onto the bed. "You brought cinnamon rolls and didn't tell me? All this time we've been up here gabbing when we could have been indulging? Come on, girl. My sugar high is calling me."

"What's with all the goats?" If Jacob were going to become accustomed to Pansy, he might as well get started learning now, where Eden couldn't overhear.

Greg grinned. "That's an interesting story. Our village qualified for two goats from Samaritan's Purse. That was about four years ago. I've lost track of how many have been born since then. A couple of dozen?"

"How can the village support so many?" These were no dwarfs like Pansy. "These beasts must eat a lot."

"They are our most precious possession next to God's word."

Surely the man jested. Jacob swung to take in Greg's expression, but it was sober. "Really?"

"You sound shocked. The goats have provided nutrition and income as well as increasing morale."

Half-naked children ran around the compound with the goats, shouting with glee.

Greg motioned toward the new solar panels, mounted on the roof of the school, a building with no walls. "These will help a lot as well, of course. We'll be able to run literacy classes into the evening, and even the young and infirm will be able to get water from the well." He grinned. "We're getting spoiled now. All the comforts of back home without the noise and expense of running the generator."

Jacob shook his head. "I don't know how you can say that. You have more than they do." He watched a goat head-butt a partially-inflated soccer ball between two children. "But compared to most in America, you live pretty simply." He'd been inside Greg and Tammy's basic cinder-block house with its thatched roof. Anyone who thought missionaries lived exotically had never experienced most of them on the ground, so to speak.

"We do keep luxuries to a minimum. Even what's very basic for us is so far beyond their reach that it's easy for them to become focused on our possessions rather than God's word. We aren't here to show off." Greg glanced at Jacob. "The goats give them hope of a better life here and now, and that's a good thing, but it's not our main purpose. We're here to learn their language and culture so we can introduce them to Jesus, their only hope for eternity."

"It's easy to forget. Maybe not for you—" Jacob poked his chin toward Greg "—but it is for me. I get pretty wrapped up in my do-good life and don't think about the people."

"It can happen here, too," Greg said quietly. "Being a missionary isn't all that glamorous. We can easily get stuck in the mundane. Wipe the daily layer of dust off every surface, scrounge up a simple meal, respond to an emergency, visit with a neighbor outside. Suddenly we realize we haven't put in the hours of translation that is currently our primary effort."

"It's easy to become distracted. To lose focus." Jacob pointed up at the solar panels. "Add dusting those to your task list. The surface needs to be clear to gather sunlight most effectively."

"There are other parallels, I'm thinking."

"Hmm?" Jacob glanced at Greg.

"Earlier you said we need to check the connections to the batteries periodically. Check the batteries to make sure they're doing their job as well. There's little point in collecting the sun's energy if we don't use it. Then the panels are just for show."

The double meaning sank into Jacob's soul. "So that's the secret, isn't it. We can't be the kind of Christians who just take in God's word and never use it. We need to keep the connections to the source tight and then do something with that spiritual energy. You're doing that, Greg."

"What you're doing makes a big difference, too. Global

Sunbeams has made an immeasurable impact on Africa, and you've been part of that. How many villages have you, personally, brought solar energy to?"

Jacob shook his head. "I've lost track. This is the seventh time I've been in the region. Sometimes it's been part of a big team. Other times have been more like this trip, just me and a helper. A guy who can drive the truck, translate, and is handy enough to help me with the installations. It's been good working with Tiago this time around."

"How many more villages are on your list?"

"Just one." Waves of homesickness welled up inside Jacob. Soon he'd see Eden and hold her in his arms. Kiss her. "I'm flying home in just a few more days."

Greg nodded in understanding. "Got a wife? Little ones?"

"A girlfriend."

"Tell me about her."

"Eden is beautiful and sweet. She loves the Lord."

"Practically perfect in every way."

Jacob's gaze caught on the group of kids — both two- and four-footed — playing with the soccer ball. "Except for the goat."

"Pardon me? I must not have heard you correctly. I thought you said goat."

"I did. Eden lives a few blocks from downtown Spokane, and she has a goat and chickens in her backyard."

"I didn't know American cities were so enlightened."

Jacob chuckled. "I'm not sure I'd jump to that conclusion. Eden would, though. We met when her goat broke through the fence and ate my presentation."

"Love at first sight?"

"It took longer than that. I was rather... angry." He cringed to remember how he'd acted toward Eden at first. So selfishly, even when he'd been fixing the fence. Really, their whole relationship had been more about making Jacob Riehl feel good than about loving Eden for herself. Why were his dreams more important than hers?

Jacob dropped his head into his hands and squeezed his eyes shut. God, what have I done? She deserves better.

He'd be home in just a few days, and he'd make it up to her. She was worth it.

"Maa."

Goat breath blasted his cheek as he jerked away from the animal staring into his eyes. Eden was definitely worth it, but could he do an about-face and become a champion of goats for her sake? God, can I learn to love a goat?

Chapter 17

"EDEN."

She wove her fingers together behind his neck, savoring the sensation of his hands caressing her shoulders, her back. Those weeks of feeling disenchanted? Certain they were destined for a breakup? Gone.

Jacob was home. Finally, finally home. Standing on her front step in the sunset, a light breeze riffling the air. Right where he belonged, holding her close.

"I missed you so much." He swept a strand of hair from her cheek, and her skin tingled from his touch. "I can't get enough of looking at you. Filling my eyes with you. Smelling your sweet scent."

He looked pretty good himself. Smelled pretty good, even with the fatigue of travel clinging to him. He'd gotten a cab home from the airport and brought his carry-on to her doorstep for all the world like he lived there. As though the two minutes it would have taken to set it inside the house next door were two more minutes he couldn't stand to be apart from her.

She understood that line of thought, even though she'd steeled herself for the opposite. He hadn't met someone else in Africa. He hadn't decided, with the benefit of weeks where she couldn't distract him, that she wasn't worth the trouble.

"I can't believe you're here," she whispered, searching his blue eyes. Her fingers caught in the curls at the nape of his neck, his hair longer than she'd ever seen it. "It seemed like forever."

He covered her mouth with his. Finally. Yet his lips teased at hers with soft kisses.

Eden slid her fingers through the tight curls and held his head in place so she could deepen the connection. His hands splayed on her back, one between her shoulders and the other above her waist. As his kiss grew hungrier, his hands tightened around her, pressing her firmly against him.

She never wanted that kiss to end. Who needed air? Who needed sleep, or food, or drink? No one. Not when they had a love like hers and Jacob's.

All too soon his lips released hers, and he buried his face in the hollow of her neck, swaying slightly. "Eden, sweetheart, I'm barely upright."

She pressed her cheek against his hair. "When did you last sleep?"

"I can't remember. In Nampula, I think. I closed my eyes a few times on the plane, but I couldn't settle into anything restful. All I could think of was this moment. Getting home. Holding you." His lips nibbled the hollow of her neck. "Kissing you."

Eden shivered at the sensation. "I missed you, too."

"I can't wait to see what you've been up to upstairs. It

sounds so nice from your emails. But first I need a date with my bed. Do you know how many times I've slept on lumpy hard mattresses or just a pad on the ground under a mosquito net?"

She shook her head slightly, and his lips grazed her ear.

"Too many. I'm exhausted clear to the bone. I'm not even sure what day it is, or if it's morning or evening."

"It's seven-thirty on Saturday evening." Or it had been, when she'd bolted out the door at the crunch of the cab's tires in the driveway. Probably a bit of time had passed since then.

"It's already early tomorrow morning in Mozambique. No wonder I'm tired."

Eden tried to disengage from his hold, but his hands did not easily release her. For that matter, hers weren't all that willing, either, even with her mind telling them they'd get another chance tomorrow. She pressed her hands against his muscular biceps and pushed away a few inches.

He stepped back far enough the evening breeze could fit between them — barely — and caught her hands in both of his. "I'll see you for church in the morning, sweetheart. Then maybe a picnic or something? I'll come up with a plan."

"Let me surprise you." Eden stretched to plant a kiss on his lips.

His grip tightened so much she might lose feeling in her fingers. His eyes darkened before he dropped another sweet kiss, his thumbs rubbing circles on hers. He took a step backward. "Good night, Eden. If I don't go now, I'm not sure I'll ever be able to." A lopsided grin lifted his lips as he released her hands and picked up his carry-on.

Eden wrapped both arms around her middle as she watched him skirt the rosebushes and make his way up the steps. Piano music poured out when he opened the door. He paused, looking back at her. She blew him a kiss, and he smiled before entering and closing her out.

The strains of Give Us Clean Hands ended abruptly, no doubt as Logan became aware that his housemate had returned. Eden hummed the melody as she went inside, the lyrics coming to her mind.

Wait. They spoke of the God of Jacob? How had she never noticed that? They mustn't have sung the song in church since she'd met Jacob Riehl. She hurried over to her computer and found the song on YouTube. After listening to it a few times, she began hunting down the scriptures that formed the basis for the lyrics.

She stared at Psalm 24:3-6 in the New Living Translation. Who may climb the mountain of the Lord? Who may stand in his holy place? Only those whose hands and hearts are pure, who do not worship idols and never tell lies. They will receive the Lord's blessing and have a right relationship with God their savior. Such people may seek you and worship in your presence, O God of Jacob.

Eden bounced gently on the exercise ball and read the verses again. Why was the God of Jacob singled out? Why not the God of Moses, or Solomon, or some other Old Testament guy? The Jacob in the Bible wasn't actually that nice of a man.

The Jacob she knew wasn't completely perfect, either, but he didn't have the grasping, impatient agenda of the original. No, her Jacob was one who sought the face of his God, who desired clean hands and a pure heart.

"I worship the God of Jacob," she told Licorice.

The cat didn't open an eye or twitch his tail.

Eden ran her fingers through his silky black coat then gathered the tom into her arms and pressed her cheek against his head. An ear twitched, tickling her nose. "He's back, kitty. He's back, and everything is going to be better than ever."

Thirteen hours in his own bed had done Jacob a world of good. It would take a few days to be fully caught up and present in this time zone, but he'd made a good start. Sitting beside Eden in church, pressed arm to arm and thigh to thigh, hearing her sing out beside him, and interlacing her fingers with his own through the sermon made the lack of sleep a minor nuisance to be ignored.

They shook hands with Pastor Tomas and Juanita. The church family swarmed around them, welcoming him back. Logan stood off to the side, talking with Linnea. His housemate had confided via email that they'd been dating. Hailey stood with pursed lips watching Logan through narrowed eyes.

Jacob held back his grin. It was good to be home. Good to worship in English amid friends and neighbors.

"You're finally here." Marietta stood in front of him, both hands on her hips. "When are you getting those panels up on the community center? We've been waiting long enough."

"Leave the boy be, Mamma." Ray Santoro nudged his mother. "He hasn't been home a day yet. He'll be on it as soon as he can." He nodded to Jacob.

"Is it so wrong to ask, Raimondo? I think not."

Ray took Marietta's arm. "If he doesn't give us news in the next few days, you go ahead and nag at him next Sunday. Today leave him be. Let him spend some time with his girl and remember he is in Spokane now, not some African desert." He gently moved his mother over a few steps. "Did you make penne with sausage for lunch today? Grace said you hinted at it."

Marietta laid her hand on her son's cheek. "You and Grazia must come for lunch, and bring some of those fresh tomatoes from your garden, si? For the salad."

"We will, Mamma." Ray glanced over his shoulder and gave a wink to Jacob and Eden.

"She's something else, isn't she?" whispered Eden. "She hasn't quite forgiven me for not marrying Roberto."

"I don't believe I've met this Roberto." Jacob slid his arm around Eden and matched his step with hers as they started down the sidewalk toward home. "Am I missing anything?"

"Not a thing. Marietta thinks her grandchildren should be married by twenty and popping out babies by twenty-one. I think Rob moved to Montana to get away from the pressure. Now she's mostly focused on Jasmine, who is all of twenty-six."

"Practically an old maid. And you're hot on her tail. But with prospects." No reaction to that hint? He bumped her with his hip. "Teasing you."

She flashed him a grin then looked away.

"So you haven't told me what the plan is for this afternoon." Hopefully she hadn't packed the agenda with too much other than kissing. Just the thought made him tighten his grip around her waist.

"I was hoping you'd be happy to hang around my place. I have lunch fixed, and I'll show you the progress on the house." She looked up at him as though unsure of his reaction. "Maybe we can cook together later. What do you think?"

In the time they'd dated, they'd avoided spending much time at her house. He might've pretended it was all about resisting temptation but, deep down, he knew there was more to it than that. Being in her space would put him face-to-face with the lifestyle she'd chosen. With the chickens.

With the goat.

"We can do something else if you'd rather."

Jacob turned her toward him on the sidewalk. "I like your plans." It was time — past time, really — for him to face Pansy. She was part of Eden's life, and he needed to accept her as such. Or the alternative. Know that he couldn't get past it.

He swept a kiss over Eden's lips. Living without this sweet woman for the rest of his life was looking like less and less of an option.

The only question remaining was whether the goat would stay or leave. Because Jacob was going nowhere.

Chapter 18

"DO YOU LIKE IT?" As she went up, Eden pointed at the stairs, which had once been covered with flattened gray carpet. Now polished oak planks were visible.

"It's looking good so far." Jacob tried to keep his mind on the house, not on Eden's backside at eye level while he climbed.

She stepped aside at the top and spread her hands.

He took that as an invitation to explore. The only room he'd been in before was the master bedroom, so it was a natural place to start. He pushed the door all the way open and caught his breath. The space couldn't have looked more different if it had been in a different house. A different neighborhood.

"You did all this?" He ran his fingers down the glossy white door trim. "It's amazing."

"I had help. Hailey peeled paper and painted. Adriana helped pick the fabrics and did the sewing."

"Adriana?" The name sounded familiar, but he couldn't place her.

"She lives around the corner with her kids, Sam and Violet. She buys goat milk from me every week."

"Oh, right. The in-your-face little girl."

Eden smiled. "That's Violet. She might not be well-named. I've never met a less shy child."

Jacob stepped further into the room. A queen-size bed with a fluffy blue spread took up most of the space. A matching window shade was halfway down behind airy white curtains.

The room looked like Eden. Fresh. Lovely. Inviting. Jacob backed out the door and peeled his gaze away from the bed. "Looks really good."

"My sisters used to share this room." Eden flung open another door. "The wallpaper was almost as bad as in the master. Covered with huge clumps of lilacs."

A twin bed sat under the window with only a low white bench beside it. She'd used the same ideas and fabrics in this one, only in a hazy hue of purple.

"You kept the bed?" Hadn't he helped haul several out to Wade's truck that day?

"Just my old twin. I, um, I bought a new one for the master." She didn't meet his gaze.

Right. Jacob opened the other door and peered into a slightly smaller room, still half-covered in garish wallpaper with marigolds all but leaping off it. He blinked and took an inadvertent step back, nearly stepping on Eden's foot.

Eden chuckled. "My sentiments exactly. I can't believe I've spent my entire life surrounded by yellow and orange."

He turned and slid a finger down her cheek. "Five years longer than required."

She nodded and chewed on her lower lip. "Guilty as charged."

The only other upstairs door stood ajar, offering him a glimpse of a bathroom with morning glories climbing the walls behind a blue toilet. He glanced again at the disarray in her childhood space and shook his head. She obviously wasn't living in the marigold room anymore. What had her parents been thinking with their decorating choices? He lingered in the master bedroom doorway, resting his eyes, while Eden started down the stairs.

Had she thought of him at all when choosing the big bed she now slept in? He could see himself living here, sleeping here, making lo—. He jogged down the steps into safer territory.

Was it safe enough? They were still alone in the house. Her house.

Licorice stretched on the sofa and opened one eye to peer at Jacob. The cat was definitely not chaperone enough to count.

The fridge door opened and closed in the kitchen. A gentle thunk sounded as Eden set something on the counter.

Jacob sucked in a deep breath and let it out slowly. Was it possible to know for sure after only two months, one of which they'd spent apart? She'd emailed daily the first week then less often, likely in response to his hurried, infrequent responses. He'd had so little time to himself, especially when they'd regrouped in the city for the next trip. He could have done better. He should have.

He bent and scratched the cat behind his ears. Licorice placed a paw on Jacob's wrist, claws slightly distended. "Don't like being touched?" Jacob murmured as the claws tightened a smidge. Talking to a cat. Who knew that would ever happen? But it helped break the weirdness he'd felt upstairs. He passed the antique dining table, stacked with papers and boxes, and entered the kitchen.

Eden looked up from chopping a cucumber at the counter and smiled at him, looking as nervous as he felt.

Okay, the mood hadn't completely dissipated. She felt it, too. Or something like it.

"Lunch is nearly ready. Do you want to eat outside or in?" Better to discuss something innocuous rather than her upstairs redecorating project any further. Seeing how he'd examined her retreat had affected her, too.

Jacob's gaze darted to the window overlooking the back porch. Uh oh. Probably checking for Pansy.

"Outside sounds good. Want me to wipe the table out there or carry anything? I may be tired, but I can be useful."

Eden let out a breath she hadn't been aware of holding. "Sure. There's a cloth by the sink."

He set both hands on her hips and kissed her neck before moving over to the sink and turning on the faucet. A moment later he went out the back door, and she caught another breath.

Today seemed so real, like a layer or two of filters had been removed. Today it was so easy to imagine him living in this little house with her, working together in her kitchen, snuggling on her sofa with Licorice draped across their laps while they ate popcorn and watched a movie. They'd snuggle upstairs in her new big bed, too, between the pale blue sheets.

Maybe it had been a bad idea to invite him to spend the day here. She'd caught the flickering emotions on his face when he'd stopped a second time in the master bedroom doorway. It wasn't just her thinking these thoughts, and that was even scarier.

But, at the same time, they needed to be here. How could Jacob understand her life if he never experienced it? She'd segmented it into four parts all too well. Jacob, work, home, church. The only part she'd shared with him was church. That was the most important, but it wasn't everything.

The screen door squeaked as Jacob entered the kitchen. He rinsed the dishcloth, wrung it out, and folded it over the faucet. No half measures for this man.

"Here." Eden slid the two plates of salad toward him, each with sliced chicken and a hardboiled egg on top. "What kind of dressing do you like? I have ranch, Italian..." She peered into the fridge.

"Of course Italian in this neighborhood." Jacob chuckled. "Good thing I like it, but ranch sounds better with this."

She nodded and set the jar beside the plates then got out silverware and glasses of iced tea. She grabbed two buns she'd picked up at the bakery yesterday and a pat of butter before helping Jacob ferry everything outside.

Pansy bleated from her pen, but Eden ignored her. She usually let the goat roam the backyard when she was home, but there'd be time enough later.

Jacob took her hand in his as they sat at the patio table. "This looks terrific, Eden. May I ask the blessing?"

"Please," she whispered then listened to him give thanks. Was it her imagination, or was his prayer more heartfelt than before Africa? Perhaps she was just more aware of everything about him today.

"These are from my hens." She sliced the hardboiled egg onto her salad and sprinkled salt and pepper on it. If today was going to be educate-a-boyfriend day, she needed to keep focused.

Jacob nodded as he followed suit. “Nice rich yolk. My sisters would say the color shows you’re treating the chickens right.”

Good. He knew the correct words. “Yes, I try. A few people in the neighborhood are good about tossing garden scraps into their run. I don’t really produce enough myself.”

“They come in when you’re not home?”

“Into the backyard, yes. Why not?”

He slathered butter on his bun. “I guess I’m not used to Bridgeview yet. No one would dream of it back home. I can’t speak for all areas of Portland, but certainly not in our part of the city.”

They wouldn’t dream of chickens and goats, either. His part of the city no doubt contained gated properties, each with an acre or two of bright green turf for the lawn maintenance companies to weed-and-feed. The goat ensured nothing green remained in Eden’s backyard. It did look rather stark when she thought of it that way, but Pansy was worth it.

“I’ve never really gardened.” Now why had she confessed that? “My backyard doesn’t get a lot of direct sunlight.”

“Peas and greens do well in shade, or so my sisters tell me.” Jacob flashed her a grin. “And hey, you’re talking to a solar architect. I make things happen with sunbeams.”

She quirked an eyebrow at him. “Like remove the entire mountain that makes up the south wall of my yard?” She snapped her fingers. “And, not so incidentally, has houses on it?”

He tapped his chin, but the crinkle around his eyes gave him away. “Marietta wouldn’t mind moving, would she? It’s for a good cause.”

Eden couldn't help the snicker that escaped. "Instead, I'll probably join her community garden next summer. She's got good light up there."

"Logan told me she hired him to build a fence around her empty lot." He glanced at Eden. "Do you know Linnea? Apparently he's been moving quickly while I was in Africa."

"I don't know her well, but she seems nice. Yes, I've seen her and Logan together a few times."

"She's doing the landscaping for Marietta's project."

Eden frowned. "What's to landscape? I thought it was raised beds for people to plant vegetables."

Jacob laid his fork across his empty plate and leaned back. "We should walk up there this afternoon and have a look. Logan said something about plants to attract butterflies and birds, too. He's got me curious."

"We could do that." A walk around the neighborhood had to be better than spending the day here alone. What had she been thinking?

She'd been thinking of Jacob meeting Pansy. Eden stood and gathered the plates. "I'll be right back." After she set them on the counter inside, she crossed the yard to Pansy's pen and opened the latch. Hmm. That felt a little loose. She should remember to tighten it later, if she could find the right screwdriver. It had to be somewhere in the house.

The goat bleated and leaned against Eden's leg.

"I know, girl. You've missed me," Eden crooned as she knelt and rubbed the goat's head and back.

Pansy shivered in delight.

"Come on. I have someone for you to meet." She gathered the goat in her arms and carried her to the back porch.

Jacob watched with unreadable eyes as she slid into the chair beside him.

"I'd really like it if you and Pansy got to know each other." She was putting him on the spot. She knew it, but it had to happen if there could be any hope for a future together. And she wanted that future. Desperately.

Enough to give up your backyard farm?

Now where had that voice come from? She'd lobbied hard and gone to every meeting the city had opened to the public. She'd helped fine-tune the livestock bylaws. The right to keep Pansy and the chickens had been hard won.

Jacob reached out a tentative hand, and Pansy shoved her head hard against it. Jacob withdrew and glanced at Eden.

Show no discomfort. "She's just saying hello."

"Uh, hi, goat." He patted her quickly.

"Pansy."

He sighed. "Hi, Pansy."

"Do you want to hold her?" Eden steeled herself against the panic in his eyes and set Pansy on his lap.

"I don't even know how to pet a cat."

"Then everything you learn can also be used on Licorice and the neighborhood dogs." How had this guy managed to grow up without pets of any kind? Wasn't withholding animals a form of child abuse? "Just rub her back. See? It soothes her." She took Jacob's limp hand and guided it.

He closed his eyes for a few seconds then gave her a tremulous smile before making the movements on his own.

Eden dared breathe. Maybe this was going to work.

Chapter 19

THE WAIST-HIGH PICKET FENCE reminded Jacob of pictures from stories. He'd never seen one in real life that he could remember. From what Logan had said, he'd expected to hear the hammer or drill, but the only sounds in the air were laughter from Marietta's house next door, the breeze rustling through the bushes along the edge of the garden lot, and the gurgle of running water somewhere nearby.

Eden's fingers tightened around his. "I'm not sure what I was expecting, but this wasn't it."

"Me, either." The lot had been cleared, terraced, and marked off in various places with sticks and strings. Several taller trees and bushes had been left in place. Jacob's gaze finally snagged on two figures off to the side. "There they are." He guided Eden beneath the arch then stuck two fingers in his mouth and whistled shrilly.

Linnea, leaning against a tree with her knees drawn to her chest, waved. Logan, who'd been stretched out on the ground, rolled to sitting and turned. "Hey, dude! Get over here. Let us show you around."

"It's looking good," Jacob ventured as they neared.

"It will look good." Linnea bounced to her feet, her thick blond braid swinging to her waist. "Right now it looks like a war zone."

Logan grinned. "You may need some imagination to see the potential. Sorry to keep you in the dark, Jake. I know you have none."

"Hey, now." Jacob cuffed Logan's shoulder. "I see lots of possibilities that you'll never dream of. You just make things out of wood." He lowered his voice and whispered, "I know the secrets of sunbeams. Unseen, yet all around us. Warming us, offering limitless power and—"

"Sounds like God," Linnea interrupted.

Jacob closed his mouth. "His creation, of course, but yes, He's given them many of His characteristics." Why had he not thought of that before?

"Jacob Riehl, speechless." Logan laughed. "Mark the date and time, ladies. This doesn't happen often."

And here he'd thought it would be good to get Logan and Eden in the same place. Jacob remembered the intense feelings he'd experienced in Eden's home. Still, they could have gone somewhere else besides here.

Eden's fingers tightened around his, and she bumped lightly against his arm. "I've rendered him speechless a time or two."

"Hard to talk when you're kissing, eh, Riehl?"

Linnea swatted Logan's arm.

"Ever tried it?" asked Eden, teasing in her voice.

Whew. She'd diverted his housemate, but the topic could come around again and bite him harder. "So, uh, tell me about this garden."

"Methinks you're trying to change the subject, dude."

Jacob pushed out a grin. "Maybe I am. But you're the one who offered."

Linnea chuckled. "He's got you there. Besides, people shouldn't kiss and tell."

He shot her a quick glance and saw her face redden.

She pointed to the rectangular areas marked out with the sticks and strings. "Marietta asked for sixteen garden beds, each four feet by twelve. Obviously those needed to be where there's the most sun, so we staked them out first."

"As you can see, the lot isn't exactly flat," Logan broke in, "so Linnea figured out how many terraces we'd need, and we built those first."

Gray basalt rocks created four levels with a concrete pad walkway up the center.

"When Logan gets the gate finished and hung, he'll start on the beds."

"What else are you doing?" asked Eden.

Linnea's eyes lit up as she waved toward the corner beside the street. "A wildlife garden. We've already got a water feature going. We both wanted to listen to that while we worked."

Jacob raised his eyebrows. Who'd been working?

"I'm developing a plan to incorporate as many shrubs and plants as I can to attract birds, butterflies, and bees."

"Marietta asked for that?" Eden sounded like she didn't quite believe it.

Linnea chuckled. "She did. Her own yard is so full of tomatoes and fava beans and that huge grape arbor she can't get anything else in it. Ray and Grace talked her into developing this lot and donating it to the community. She agreed, but only because she already had a gate on this side." She pointed toward the tall mesh fence separating the properties. “She’ll keep an eye on things as long as she’s alive. Guaranteed.”

“Yeah, I can’t see her relinquishing control.” Eden grinned.

“She’s over here constantly micro-managing the whole project.” Logan sighed. “She’s changed her mind about ten times as to where she wants the gazebo to go.”

“Gazebo?” Jacob quirked his eyebrows.

“Oh, she’s thinking of lots of construction projects to keep me busy in my spare time.”

Jacob bit back a grin. “You didn’t look all that busy when we arrived.”

Linnea’s face reddened as Logan shook his head, his eyes glimmering with mirth. “Everyone needs a day of rest occasionally.”

“Not a bad idea,” said Eden. “It’s hard to take one off completely when you work fulltime, though.”

“Marietta doesn’t care if it takes until the snow flies to get everything done.” Logan glanced at Linnea. “She just wants it ready for spring planting.”

Jacob gestured between them. “Is she trying to set you two up?”

How much redder could Linnea’s face turn, anyway? Logan reached for her hand. “Maybe. We’re not asking any questions.”

Jacob chuckled.

“Marietta gets pushy when thwarted.” Eden rolled her eyes. “Ask me how I know.”

Linnea giggled, but Logan tipped his head and regarded Eden. “Okay, I’ll bite. How do you know?”

“She’s been pushing her grandson Roberto at me since we were about twelve.”

Logan grinned. "So it is possible to resist Marietta. But it is really mean of you to break Roberto's heart. He's probably much nicer than Jacob here. He's Italian, right? How much more romantic can a man be?"

"You're not so Italian yourself," Jacob growled. "Shall I start giving Linnea a list of your faults? Because I can."

Logan held up both hands, his eyes dancing. "Oh, please, no. Let her find out for herself. I mean, she already knows I'm not Italian, and she still likes me."

Linnea's face, which had almost faded to its natural color, darkened again.

"You guys are mean." Eden let go of Jacob's hand and linked arms with Linnea. "Show me your garden plans. I could use some ideas for my own yard." The women moved off, heads together as they talked.

Jacob stared after them. Ideas for her yard? Was there anything Pansy didn't eat? And if the goat didn't get there first, the chickens scratched it up. Eden's entire backyard looked like a nuclear wasteland.

"Didn't mean to embarrass you, dude." Logan's elbow found Jacob's ribs.

"No harm done." Jacob pulled his attention back to his housemate. "What are you doing for electrical in here? Is the fountain wired?"

"We picked up a solar pump for it. And the gazebo will have a solar panel on it to run a small-load circuit for lights and such."

Jacob clouted his friend on the shoulder. "Good to see you can be taught."

Eden arranged several kinds of crackers on a small platter and set a dish of herbed goat cheese in the middle. Then she leaned both hands on the counter and closed her eyes. "God?" she whispered. "Sometimes I believe You brought Jacob into my life, and other times I'm just not sure." He hadn't looked very comfortable petting Pansy earlier, handing her back to Eden in under a minute. He was trying. She'd give him that. But was it enough? Yet the longer they lived this charade, the harder a breakup would be. "God, I need a real answer, and I need it soon."

"May I use your restroom?"

Eden's eyes sprang open. Linnea stood framed in the door to the back porch. "Sure. It's right through here." She pointed out the painted wooden door beside the harvest gold refrigerator. Once she finished upstairs she was going to have to tackle this level. But renovating the kitchen and bringing it into the third millennium was going to be expensive, to say nothing of time consuming. Life consuming.

The men's voices and laughter came through the screen door as Linnea returned to the kitchen. "May I help with something?"

"Sure. There's a pitcher of iced tea in the fridge, if you want to get that." Eden pulled out a tray and set her platter on it, along with four tall glasses.

"Your home is adorable." Linnea set the pitcher on the counter. "I just love the older houses in Bridgeview.

Eden shook her head. "It's so dated. I've only started trying to fix it up. It's overwhelming."

Linnea glanced through to the dining area and the living room beyond. "I'm sure."

Eden followed her gaze across the clutter. "Not that you see evidence of any work being done." She glanced through the window to the back porch. The guys could wait another five minutes, right? "Come on. Let me show you." She led the way up the stairs.

"Oh, this is serene!" Linnea pressed her hand over her heart as she peered into the master bedroom. "You have excellent taste."

"Thanks." Eden couldn't help the smile poking at her cheeks. "I've had a lot of help from my friends, especially Hailey and Adriana." Would they really stick with her through an entire house reno?

"Adriana is amazing, isn't she?" Linnea turned and followed Eden to the next bedroom. "I love what you've done here, too."

"You should have seen them before." Eden pointed into her former space. "This gives you a sample."

"Wow." Linnea shook her head. "The time had come, all right."

"And the upstairs bath." Eden opened the door. "I don't think I can afford to replace all the fixtures, so I'm not sure what to do."

Linnea entered and looked around. "This isn't so bad. I think if you got rid of the wallpaper and updated the brass fixtures, you'd find the powder blue would be fine. It's not so different from the aqua in your bedroom."

Hmm. Eden pressed a finger to her chin. "You might be right. It's hard to look past the garish design."

"They sure did love pattern."

"And you didn't see the other two rooms before." Eden laughed. "The house had been recently redone when my parents bought it in 1986. They never changed a thing."

"Well, I think the bones of it are solid, and you've got a good eye for decorating." Linnea followed her down the stairs and back into the kitchen.

Eden glanced through the screen door as she picked up the tray. “I’m sure you can’t say the same about the backyard.”

“Just because I’m a landscaper doesn’t mean I feel the need to make over everyone’s space.” Out on the porch, Linnea continued. “I imagine it’s hard to find anything a goat doesn’t eat or destroy.”

Jacob’s voice cut off in mid-sentence.

“Goats do have a reputation.” Eden didn’t dare look at him. She set down the tray, took the pitcher from her friend, and began pouring tea. “And Pansy is not the exception.”

“I believe in making spaces useful for the task they are meant to perform.” Linnea picked up a glass and sat in the chair next to Logan. “Some people need a relaxing oasis, some people need a play area for children, some need to maximize vegetable production.” She shrugged. “You’ve got a backyard farm, so your choices are different again.”

Eden sank into the seat beside Jacob and slid her hand over his on the arm of his chair. He didn’t respond, and she didn’t glance his way in an attempt to read his face. “You’re right. My animals are a choice. They don’t share the space well with a garden of any sort. I do have a few rosebushes and other flowers up front, though.”

She resisted the impulse to touch the tattoo. All the changes she’d made and contemplated felt disloyal to her parents’ memory. Had her mom really loved all the garish patterns and colors in the house, or was it just too much hassle to change anything? Mom had worked full-time as a legal secretary. Maybe the house had simply never hit the top of the priority list. Maybe Eden wasn’t sending judgment back in time.

"If you're looking for more decorating ideas, though, I hear they're doing open houses in Kendall Yards." Linnea sipped her iced tea.

"That's a thought." Though she wasn't into ultra-modern.

Jacob's hand turned over and his fingers clasped hers. "That sounds fun. They're committed to the most sustainable designs over there. It's an amazing development. Want to check it out next Saturday?"

She thought about the coming week. "Sure. I can't think of any reason that won't work."

"Sounds good."

Eden pointed at the platter on the table. "I brought out some homemade cheese. Want to give it a try?" She met Jacob's gaze.

His face tightened slightly before he gave her a small smile. "Sure." After spreading a tiny bit on a cracker and tasting it, he glanced back at her. "It's good."

He didn't sound convinced. She was hoping for something a bit more enthusiastic.

Linnea almost made up for it. "Oh, I love this. So tasty. What's in it? Oregano? Rosemary? It's from Pansy's milk, right?"

"Correct on all counts. I've been experimenting. Adriana has ordered a batch of it for her dinner party." The one she had yet to mention to Jacob.

"Which reminds me." Logan spread cheese on several crackers. "Linnea and I are going to that party." He glanced at Jacob. "She said she'd hold two seats for you guys if you wanted them."

"For when?"

"Next Sunday. Six-thirty."

"Want to, Eden?" Jacob leaned back in his chair, hands linked behind his head, not having had a second taste of the goat cheese.

Eden squelched her disappointment but gave him a bright smile. "Sure. I'll milk a bit early. I can do that."

"Then we're in." Jacob's grin did not quite reach his eyes.

Eden couldn't help but wonder if their relationship was a ticking time bomb. Were they ever going to see eye-to-eye on Pansy?

Chapter 20

THEY DRIFTED THROUGH THE next week like before he'd gone to Mozambique, seeing each other after work, but not at home. Jacob tried to tell himself it was to resist temptation at being alone in a private place, but he wasn't kidding himself. For him, it was all about avoiding Pansy. But it was a good sign Eden wanted to tour the Kendall Yards complex, right? There was still hope.

Eden's front door opened, and she slipped out wearing a pretty sundress, hair tumbling to her shoulders. Her smile brightened when she saw him standing beside his car.

Jacob rested his hands on her hips and gave her a kiss before opening the car door for her. A few minutes later they'd circled around to the bridge, crossed the river, and driven into the new development. His lungs expanded at the view. He preferred the bridge from this angle.

Eden slid her hand into his as they strolled up the walkway to the sales office. She glanced all around them but didn't say anything. That was okay. She seemed open to the possibilities.

"Good morning!" The forty-something man behind the desk stood. "I'm Vern Haskell. May I show you our units?"

Jacob shook the man's hand. "I'm Jacob Riehl, and this is my girlfriend, Eden Andrusek. We'd love to have a tour."

"Excellent. Young couple like yourselves, you're probably looking for a three-bedroom, right? Thinking of leasing or buying?"

He felt Eden's hand clench in his. "Just looking at possibilities, at the moment."

"Well, let me tell you all about our sustainable building practices." Vern came around the desk and opened the door, escorting them back into the summer morning. "Our company is a trend-setter in every way. Would you like to see one of the loft-style town homes?"

Jacob glanced at Eden, but she wasn't looking at him. What was she thinking? It didn't matter at the moment. As soon as she saw the design possibilities, she'd get into the spirit of the day. "Sure. We'd like to see several different options."

Vern keyed a code into a door plate in the middle of angular town homes. "This row has parking from the rear at the basement level, which offers more glass in the main living quarters. This particular unit has walnut cabinetry and granite countertops paired with stainless appliances, with all three bedrooms and two full baths upstairs." He gestured to a door. "Plus a powder room on this level."

The view pulled Jacob across the dark hardwood floor and, with him, Eden. He slid his arm around her and pointed down across the river. "Look at that. You can see Bridgeview from here." He slid open the patio door to the small deck and tugged her outside. "And look how far you can see. What do you think?"

She chewed on her bottom lip. "There's a good view," she said at last.

Score! Jacob turned back into the unit and glanced over the soothing ultra-contemporary finish. "Let's see the upstairs." He followed her up the steps. All three bedrooms sported large windows, the master with the same view over the river. He could really get used to this. "Like it?"

Eden drew her arms around her waist. "This isn't really my style at all."

Oh. He thought about her house, a wreck of eighties' decorating. No wonder this was a bit of a shock, but she was doing well pulling it into the current millennium. "There are other options. They do more traditional, as well."

"Okay." She gave him a tremulous smile, and he dropped a kiss onto her pretty pink lips.

"Come on." He held out his hand to her, and she took it. Eden was meeting him halfway, at least exploring the option.

The semi-detached house Vern showed them next seemed perfect. Warmer cabinetry, softer colors, though still neutral. And a bit more space, as well. Nothing like the house he'd grown up in, of course, but a good starter home for the area. It should've put a smile on Eden's face, but it didn't seem to.

"I've got one more just around the block." Vern looked from one to the other. "It's fully detached with four bedrooms and four baths. Three-car garage."

Eden's mouth drew into a line, and Jacob shook his head. "Thanks, Vern. I think that's enough for today. You've definitely given us something to think about, though. We appreciate your time."

"Units around here move quickly." Vern rocked back on his heels. "We often have a wait list of a year or more. If you're looking at custom, we may need even longer. That second home I showed you is available now, but it could be snapped up any minute. I had someone looking at it yesterday who seemed quite serious."

Jacob reached for Vern's hand and gave it a firm shake. "Thanks for the information. We'll be in touch if we want to move ahead." He followed Eden to the car and opened the passenger door for her before rounding the vehicle and sliding in the other side. A glance across the interior revealed her blankly staring out the window.

He started the car and pulled away from the curb, leaving Vern still standing on the sidewalk, hands shoved in his pockets. "What did you think?" he asked at last.

"It was interesting."

"That's all?"

"I'd hoped to get some ideas of what I could do with the rest of my house, but nothing really caught my eye."

"To freshen it up for sale, or what?"

She swiveled to look at him. "I don't have any plans to sell. It's been my home for my entire life, and I own it free and clear. Why would I sell it?"

He'd need to tread very carefully here. "I wasn't sure what your plans were. You never said."

Eden's arms crossed over her chest. "There are thousands of things I don't plan to do that I haven't mentioned. How could I know you'd think I might want to do something, just because I never said I didn't?"

His head hurt. "Then why did we go today?"

"I don't know why you went. I went because Linnea suggested I might get some decorating ideas there. Which she said when you and Logan were there, so I didn't think it was a big mystery."

"Oh." Jacob swallowed hard. When he sent his mind back

to rake through that memory, those words did seem familiar. He'd jumped to a conclusion. A big one. A wrong, messy one.

"Kendall Yards isn't open to chickens, let alone goats. And besides, it's just not my style." She narrowed her gaze as she watched him. "I suppose it is yours, though."

Jacob's gut clenched. Was this the end of the road? It couldn't be. He loved Eden, just not her goat. Just not her house. Could he still claim love in that case? He needed time. Time to think. Time to pray. Yeah, he'd had an entire month in Mozambique. He'd decided she was worth it. That he could do it, whatever it was.

He managed a smile for Eden. "I could go either way. I do like the more modern lines, but there's something to be said for older homes, too."

The ride home was quiet. Eden clenched her jaw and blinked back tears. Whom had she been trying to fool? She and Jacob weren't meant to be.

When he pulled into the driveway, she popped the car door open without waiting for him and managed a semblance of a smile. "Talk to you later."

"I'll call." But his voice didn't hold the warmth and confidence it usually did.

She skirted around the rosebushes on the way to her front door. I miss you, Mom. I could sure use a mother-daughter chat right now. Someone to talk to whom I know has my back.

Inside the house, Eden leaned against the closed front door. Her parents were gone. Her sisters. She thought of calling Hailey, but did she really want to dump everything on her friend and deal with the added drama every conversation with Hailey brought? No. She scooped Licorice into her arms and squished him tight as hot tears soaked his fur.

Hadn't she had a full life before meeting Jacob Riehl? She could have a full life again. Couldn't she? Eden felt his arms around her, relived his passionate kisses, the deepness of his blue eyes as he spoke words of love to her.

It was all a lie. He didn't love her. He wanted to change her into someone else.

But didn't she want to change him, too?

Eden's jaw quivered. "Oh, kitty. Human life is so complicated. Be glad you're a cat." She nuzzled Licorice's fur then set him down on the sofa. He stretched every sinew of his long black body.

Now what? The hazy August afternoon stretched ahead of her. She'd finished stripping the wallpaper in her old bedroom during the week. Might as well start on the morning glory paper in the upstairs bath. But once in her room, she flopped onto the large bed on her back, staring up at the white ceiling.

The entire time she'd removed the old and brought in the new, she'd been dreaming of sharing this space with Jacob while he'd been dreaming of a master suite in Kendall Yards with miles of white carpet and a walk-in closet bigger than her old bedroom.

He came from money.

Eden didn't.

He was a member of Team Goldfish.

She came from Team Goat.

How could she ever have thought they could make this work, when right from the start Pansy had come between them? She should have known better than to lose her heart to Jacob. It had been too good to last.

Enough. She kicked off her heeled sandals, stepped out of her sundress, and put on her jean shorts and a tank.

Time to peel wallpaper.

A while later she heard Jacob's car leave the house next door. Where was he off to? She glanced at her phone, but he hadn't left a text.

This was the beginning of the end. She could feel the weight in her heart. Was it her? Should she be willing to give up Pansy, the chickens, her home, everything if she truly loved Jacob? Was it fair to think he'd step into her life, making all the sacrifices while she made none?

A guy like Rob Santoro wouldn't dream of wanting to change her. Not that she loved him. He hadn't been back in Spokane since that deck party last year at Marietta's, and he'd never made her heart leap. Not like it did for Jacob.

"Lord? How do I know if it's just me being selfish and stubborn, or whether I need to let Jacob go?"

The room was not lit by a lightning flash from on high.

She would have taken any sign, but a cat cleaning his ears with repeated swipes of a black paw didn't count.

Chapter 21

JAKEY!" CHELSEA REACHED OUT the door of her home and crushed him to her. "What are you doing here? Why didn't you call?" She peered past him. "Where's Eden?"

Jacob forced a smile. "She's in Spokane. I needed some thinking time, so I went for a drive and, before I knew it, I was on my way to Galena Landing. Hope you don't mind."

"You're not driving back tonight, are you? It's too late. Stay with us?"

"I didn't bring anything. Not even a toothbrush."

His sister swept that aside as she pulled him into her little house. "Doesn't matter. We can scrounge up something. Keanan, look what I found on the doorstep."

Jacob's brother-in-law stilled the strings on the guitar he'd been playing. "Jacob!" He set the instrument down then crossed the small space to shake Jacob's hand and thump him on the back. "You are welcome here always."

"Thanks."

Chelsea pointed at an easy chair as she perched on a tall stool at the island. "Are you here to tell us you proposed to Eden? Mom and Dad will be thrilled."

Jacob shook his head. "No." He looked from Chelsea to Keanan then back again. "I don't know what to do, Chels. I thought we were making progress, I really did. I thought I loved her."

"Uh oh." Chelsea exchanged a glance with her husband. "This doesn't sound good. What happened?"

"It's the goat."

"The what?" Chelsea laughed out loud but straightened her face when she took a closer look at him. "You're serious."

Jacob nodded. "I just can't get over the goat. I spent a month in Mozambique and saw hundreds of them. Thousands, probably. They seem to fit there. They provide food and income. But what good does Pansy do?"

Keanan's green eyes bored into Jacob's. "They provide the same thing in the United States."

"Eden sells goat milk and cheese to her neighbors, doesn't she?" Chelsea braced her hands on her knees. "That's food and income both."

"There's not much left after expenses are paid. Pansy is really a pet. One that destroys the backyard and ties Eden down to twice-a-day milking."

"So you resent the time Eden spends with her goat?" asked Chelsea.

"I hadn't thought of it exactly like that." Jacob ran his hands through his hair. How could he compete with a goat? Why should he even want to? The memory of sweet kisses rocked his soul. Yeah. That's why.

He surged to his feet. "I took her to see the new development at Kendall Yards this morning. I was hoping she might see the possibilities of buying a place there, but she isn't even interested. They don't allow goats or chickens." He shook his head. "Of course they don't. Why would they?"

Keanan and Chelsea exchanged a look.

"What? Is it so wrong to want to love a woman who loves you more than she loves her goat?"

Chelsea's eyes gleamed and a little smile poked at her cheeks.

Jacob pointed a finger at her. "Don't even start with me, or I'm leaving right now."

She held up both hands, palms toward him. "Love is patient and kind. Love is not jealous or boastful or proud or rude. It does not demand its own way. It is not irritable..."

He glared at her. "Your point is?"

"Love does not demand its own way."

"I heard you the first time."

Chelsea's eyebrows rose as she met his gaze. "It bears repeating."

"Love keeps no record of being wronged," Keanan broke in. "It does not rejoice about injustice but rejoices whenever the truth wins out. Love never gives up, never loses faith, is always hopeful, and endures through every circumstance."

Great. Now they were tag-teaming him. "Are you two quite finished?"

Chelsea grinned. "There's more, if you want to look up the thirteenth chapter of First Corinthians."

"Look, I know all that, okay? I memorized it in school same as you did, Chels. It doesn't help. What I don't know is if I'm supposed to love Eden that way. Maybe I haven't met the right woman yet."

"What would she be like?" Keanan asked mildly.

Jacob ran his fingers through his hair again as Eden's face swam into his vision, her sweet lips turned up to his, her blue eyes looking at him with love. "She'd be pretty, and have a sense of humor. She'd love Jesus, and she'd love me. She'd be fun to be with, and enjoy hiking and the outdoors. She'd like kids. She'd appreciate good food and be creative and smart."

Chelsea raised her eyebrows. "Sounds a lot like Eden."

Jacob narrowed his gaze at her. "She'd have a flower garden and a vegetable garden and she wouldn't have a goat."

"Is the problem Pansy, or is it you?"

Jacob swung to look at his brother-in-law. Silence stretched for a long moment. "I don't know," he said at last. "I wish I did."

"I'd like to stay and visit." Keanan got to his feet. "But I have some chores to do. Want to come with me?"

Jacob shrugged. "Okay." He followed Keanan out the door. "What are we doing?"

"Milking the goats. I'd like to teach you how."

Jacob stopped in the middle of the path. "That's not even funny."

"It wasn't meant to be." Keanan turned and looked at him. "It's one of my chores this week, and I think it would do you some good to handle them. Have you helped Eden with Pansy?"

"No, I haven't." Why was everyone ganging up on him? "I touched her for the first time a few days ago."

Keanan swung his head in invitation. "Come on then."

"I don't get what the big thing is about goats." Jacob's gut churned as he fell into step beside his brother-in-law. "Even in the Bible, they are the bad guys. Doesn't Jesus say He'll separate the sheep from the goats? Sheep go to heaven. Goats don't."

"What did God say when He made them?"

"Huh?"

"In Genesis."

Jacob thought for a second. "It doesn't exactly mention them there, that I remember."

"Does it say, 'God made all sorts of wild animals, livestock, and small animals, each able to produce offspring of the same kind. And God saw that a few of them were good.'?"

"Well, no. But the tune changes in the New Testament."

"Goats are known for being somewhat more stubborn and aggressive than sheep," Keanan went on. "They will eat anything, whether its garbage or not, and they like to look down on everything."

Like Pansy on the roof of her shed.

"They're not very obedient. Sheep, on the other hand, follow their shepherd and need a protector."

"Seems like I remember that sheep go astray, too."

"They sure do." Keanan pushed open the door to the barn. "We've got an entire flock here, so ask me how I know."

Jacob followed him into the brightly-lit space. Those solar panels on the roof were certainly doing their job.

Keanan turned to him. "Here's the thing. There's a lot of goat in every one of us. Willful, disobedient, proud. That's why we need Jesus."

Willful. Disobedient. Proud. Had his brother-in-law just described Jacob?

Jacob's car hadn't come back last night. Eden had checked out the window multiple times, including at two and four-forty in the morning when she couldn't sleep. Where was he? Was he okay? If she had Logan's number, she might have called, but she didn't.

Besides, if Jacob wanted her to know where he was, he would've told her.

That hurt.

How could she go to church today? Hailey would ask where Jacob was. She didn't have an answer, and Hailey wouldn't be the only one with questions.

This was crazy. Bridgeview Bible had been her home church since she was a child. She wasn't staying away because of Jacob. She hadn't done anything wrong. Other than maybe falling in love with the wrong man, but even after nearly twenty hours without word from him, she couldn't quite believe that.

She applied her makeup carefully, slipped on her favorite sundress, and walked the six blocks. The sun shone and a gentle breeze riffled her hair. It was good to be alive, whether Jacob was in her life or not.

Logan began to play the distinctive introduction to Cornerstone by Hillsong just as Eden slid into the bench beside Hailey. She gave her friend a small smile and allowed her mind to prepare for worship.

My hope is built on nothing less than Jesus' blood and righteousness. I dare not trust the sweetest frame, but wholly lean on Jesus' name.

She took a deep breath and joined the exultation of the updated chorus to the age-old hymn. It was true that Jesus was Lord of all, no matter what happened. And He was all that mattered. He'd put her wounded heart back together if needed. She could trust Him.

"Where's Jacob?" whispered Hailey into the first lull.

Eden smiled at her friend. "Not sure," she whispered back.

"Everything okay?"

"Yep." And, somehow, it was.

After the service was over, she threaded her way to Logan. "Hey."

"Hi, Eden." His jaw twitched. "By the look on your face, I'd say you haven't heard from him."

"You'd be right. Just tell me, is he okay?"

"Yeah, I think so. He called me from his sister's house last night."

Eden pulled back. "His sister? At Green Acres Farm? He didn't say anything about driving all the way there."

"I don't think he planned to. He was upset." Logan held up both hands. "I don't need to know anything."

"I couldn't tell you what happened if I tried." That wasn't entirely true. "It's that I love living in my little house in Bridgeview with a goat in the backyard."

"I figured he was going to have to face that sooner or later."

He faced it by running off to Galena Landing? But his sisters were sensible, and they had goats at the farm. Where they belonged, in Jacob's estimation. Still, he could be getting support from worse places.

Logan's phone beeped with an incoming text, and he swiped it on. "Jacob." He glanced at Eden. "On his way home."

Her own cell remained silent. Hopefully no news was good news. They had a date to Adriana's tonight along with half the people they knew. Logan and Linnea. Wade and Rebekah. She couldn't go without him when he'd been the one to confirm with Adriana, could she? Surely if he were going to bow out — if he were going to break up with her — he'd let her know.

Had it really come to that?

"I'm not sure I ever said a proper thanks to you for dinner last Sunday. Linnea and I had a good time."

Eden managed a smile. "Thanks for coming. I've been a loner for too long, keeping to myself."

Hailey's hip bumped her own. "Hey now. Not quite a loner."

"No, not quite." Eden linked arms with her. "I've always had friends."

Logan's gaze went past them. "I need to get going." He focused back on Eden. "Assuming we'll see you guys at Adriana's later?"

"As far as I know."

"Good. See you then." He grinned and excused himself.

Hailey tugged Eden aside. "What's going on with Jacob?"

"I'm not sure, honestly. I think he's finally coming to grips with the fact that I have a goat. And he's not a fan."

"Really? How could he possibly not love Pansy?"

"That's where you and I are the same. And he's not."

Chapter 22

IT WAS LATE AFTERNOON WHEN Jacob pulled into the driveway of the rental Victorian in Bridgeview. He pressed the button to shut off the car and stared at Eden's vehicle and little house. She was probably home.

He lowered his forehead to the steering wheel. This is it, God. I'm not completely convinced I can go through with this.

He was still wearing yesterday's clothes. He should go have a shower first. Get changed. But there was no point in getting clean before touching a goat when he'd certainly need one afterward. Were they still having dinner at Adriana's? Would Eden forgive him for running away on her? Or maybe she'd written him off already.

He should've called. Texted, at least, but he'd had no idea what to say.

Still didn't.

Jacob pushed the car door open. It wasn't going to get any easier by putting it off. He stood for a moment, massaging his scalp then trying to smooth his hair back in place.

Help me, Lord. If we're in Your will, please help us.

Eden's rosebushes were covered in pink blossoms, as sweet and fresh as she was. He inhaled their fragrance then knocked on her front door. No answer.

He heard Pansy bleat from the backyard, so he walked around to the gate, heart hammering. As he passed through and latched it behind him, the little goat crow-hopped toward him.

Pansy was a lot smaller than most of the goats Keanan had introduced him to last night. No horns to get her point across. She was kind of cute in a Facebook meme kind of way. The goat butted a partially-deflated ball, and it bounced toward him, sending his mind back to the shade of Greg's tree in Mozambique. She wanted to play.

Jacob nudged the ball back at her with his foot. Wow, he hadn't played soccer in eons. There must be some neighborhood league he could join.

Thinking of staying in Bridgeview, Jake?

He raised his eyebrows at the goat, not that Pansy had spoken. "Maybe I am." Jacob danced closer, scooped the ball away from the goat's lowered head, and bopped it between his feet. The thing could use some serious air.

Pansy pounced, and Jacob bumped the ball behind his feet so the goat missed.

"Maa."

"Jacob?"

He looked toward the back porch, where Eden stood in shorts and a tank top, strands of hair loose from her ponytail, dirt smudged on her hands and arms. He couldn't help staring. She was gorgeous.

He spread his hands. "Hi, Eden."

Pansy butted his kneecap, nearly sending him to the ground. She had a wicked bony head.

Jacob's shifting feet kept the ball away from the goat, knowing what to do without his mind weighing in. Good thing, because his brain was in slo mo watching Eden come down the few steps to the yard.

"What are you doing?"

"Playing with Pansy. What does it look like?"

Eden's fists found her hips. "But..." Her puzzled gaze bounced between him and the goat just as the ball did.

Jacob gave the ball a solid punt to the other side of the yard, and Pansy leaped after it like a bumbling puppy. He felt the lure of Eden's eyes tugging him closer until he stood within reach of her.

Eden took his outstretched hands but kept her distance. "What's going on, Jacob?"

That question probably covered a multitude of topics. "I'm sorry for... everything. And I love you."

The ball hit the back of his knees. The goat rammed half a second later, propelling him forward. "Ouch, Pansy. Take it easy." And yet, thank you. Because now he was close enough to Eden to fill his senses with her perfume and feel the heat from her body so close to his.

Jacob swept the hair that had fallen forward behind her ear. Her blue eyes gazed at him from only a few inches away. "I'm sorry, Eden. I jumped to conclusions yesterday. Conclusions I wanted to believe, that you might have the same goals I did. I've been trying to pretend that Pansy was a passing fancy for you, and you'd get your backyard farm out of your system, and we could live the kind of upscale urban life I've always been accustomed to." Was he proposing? No. He'd better not say those words until he knew for sure they were on the same page.

Her eyes focused somewhere in the neighborhood of his

top shirt button as she bit her lip. "She's not a passing fancy." The words were barely a whisper.

"I know."

"So where does that leave us?"

Jacob tucked one hand under her chin and tipped it up until her eyes met his. "It leaves me learning how to truly appreciate Pansy. Unless you've been having second thoughts about us."

A glimmer of hope shone in her eyes. "Really?"

"I knew who you were from the moment I first met you." The vision of Pansy in his backyard, chewing on those papers, brought a twitch to his lips. "It was unbelievably arrogant of me to think you'd change your entire lifestyle for me."

Eden said nothing, just stared at him, her lips slightly parted.

He resisted the nearly overwhelming urge to bend those few inches and kiss her. "We have three choices. We either part ways, or you change, or I change." He rubbed his thumb across her cheek. "I'm not willing for the first one, and I'm not asking the second one of you."

"Logan said you went to Green Acres."

Jacob nodded. "I stayed over with Chelsea and Keanan last night. Keanan took me out to the barn and taught me how to milk the goats. Maybe he talked some sense into me."

"You milked a goat? Really?"

He raised his eyebrows. "Three of them."

"I hope this isn't some kind of joke. When you left here yesterday, I didn't think anything like this could ever happen."

His face morphed into a half smile. "Me, either. I was angry. Selfish. I wanted you to change into the woman I thought I deserved."

Her hands disengaged from his and settled on his hips.

Now that was a major victory. "I learned something, Eden. God showed me that I needed to become the man you deserve."

Her hands slid up and down his ribcage as her eyes searched his.

Jacob's skin tingled with awareness. "May I kiss you, Eden?" he whispered.

She grabbed both sides of his shirt collar and pulled him closer. "Not if I kiss you first."

Adriana pressed her lips to one of Eden's cheeks then the other. "Come in, come in! I'll just take the goat cheese from you so I can finish up the dessert."

The goat cheese. Oh, no. "I forgot it. I'll be back in ten minutes." Not that Eden wanted to miss any of the party. "I had it ready and even left myself a note on the counter." She'd been too busy dreaming about a future with Jacob to think.

"Want me to go?" he asked. "I can jog over. It won't take long."

Violet bounced up and down, nearly ramming into Eden's chin. "I'll go! I'll go! I can do it."

Eden smiled at the girl. "I don't think you're tall enough to reach the gate latch." She nudged at Jacob's ribs, and he shifted away from the door. "I'm the one who forgot. I'll go."

"I'm tall enough," said Sam. "I can take my bike and my backpack."

Adriana tousled her son's hair and met Eden's gaze. "Sam

probably would be the quickest, unless you don't want him going in your house when you're not home."

"I could so reach the latch." Violet crossed her arms over her chest and glowered at Eden.

Speaking of trust. "Are you sure you don't mind, Sam? It's in a pint jar in the fridge door, and it's labeled with your mom's name."

Violet's jaw jutted forward. "I can read Mom's name even though it's long. It's spelled A-D-R—"

"Violet, enough." Adriana rested her hand on her daughter's shoulder. "Sam is going. Leave everything just as you found it, Sam. Make sure the fridge door is shut."

Sam flashed a grin at Eden and stuck his tongue out at his sister.

"It's not fair," whined Violet as Sam shrugged into his backpack and reached for his bike helmet. "I want to go."

Adriana turned Violet into the kitchen. "I need your help with the pasta machine."

"I don't want to."

"Then go read in your room until dinner. Sorry about that, Eden and Jacob. Come on in. If you'd like a glass of mead, help yourself." She pointed at a couple of bottles open on a small counter, surrounded by several wine glasses. "Logan and Linnea and Wade and Rebekah are out on the deck. It's probably Ropers' last evening out before the baby. They're due next week."

"I thought she looked ready to pop at church this morning." Eden grinned. "Is anyone else coming?"

Adriana nodded. "Francesca and Tad, but their babysitter is late. They'll be along shortly."

"I could play with Tieri and Luca." Violet parked her hands on her hips.

"Sweetie, we talked about this. They need a sitter at their house because the kids are little and need to go to bed soon. Now, if you aren't going to help with the pasta, please leave the kitchen."

Violet glowered but did as she was told.

Adriana shook her head. "Seven and going on seventeen."

"Maybe I can help with the pasta. It's my fault Sam isn't here."

"No, it's okay. I've got it. Nearly everything is ready. Just a few last minute things."

Sitting with adult friends on the deck overlooking the river with a glass of mead in her hands sounded inviting. But when someone needed help but was too proud to ask for it... Eden washed her hands at the sink. "I'm not leaving the kitchen. Put me to work."

"But I can't—"

"Me, too," said Jacob. "What can I do?"

Adriana looked between them and sighed. "Are you sure? Violet had a hissy fit this afternoon and set me behind."

"Absolutely certain." Jacob dried his hands. "What's this with the pasta?"

"Easier to show than tell." Adriana glanced at Eden. "Would you mind giving the sauce a stir and grating some of that Viejo cheese from Quillisascut in the fridge drawer? It's similar to a Romano."

"Sure, I can do that." She listened to Adriana explaining the pasta maker to Jacob as they cranked the dough between the rollers.

"Do you often have people over?" asked Jacob.

"As often as I can." Their hostess sighed. "I'd like to do it more, but it's a lot of work, especially when Violet gets this way. And, I shouldn't say it, but I can't afford to put on a big spread every week, much as I'd love to. I love having company."

"You could totally charge for dinners." Eden glanced around the large, magazine-worthy kitchen, a far cry from her own. "Not only that, but why not make helping with dinner prep part of the experience?"

"Oh, I couldn't do that. Who'd pay to make their own dinner?" A blush crept up Adriana's cheek. "Or have me cook?"

"I'm serious, Adriana. You're good at this. Educate people while you're at it. Tell them the origins of the ingredients. Get them excited about local growers and gardening. Teach them the methods."

"But..." Adriana looked over at Eden. "Do you really think so?"

"Totally. I'm sure you can sell the experience, not just the food."

"I'd have paid for this." Jacob flipped long strands of pasta into the waiting flour.

"No, I couldn't possibly."

He grinned. "Why not? You'd be selling a cooking class and a gourmet meal."

"You could advertise in the Spokesman-Review." Eden set the grater aside. "Is this enough cheese?"

"A bit more, I think?" Adriana rolled another ball of dough into the pasta machine. "Do you guys really think that would be a good move? I could use more income with the kids growing so quickly. I'm thankful Stephan had a good life insurance policy and the house is paid for. But my diploma in business management is over ten years old, and I don't have the experience to get a job in that field, even if it weren't so outdated. Besides, the kids need me around."

Sam came in and set down his backpack, face flushed. "I pedaled as hard as I could. Was I fast enough?"

"You sure were. Thank you. Can you set the jar on the counter?" Adriana glanced at Jacob. "Do you mind finishing this part? Or maybe Sam can wash up and help you."

"It's men's work." Sam headed to the sink. "We can do this better than women."

Jacob grinned at the boy. "I'm happy to settle for doing it as well as your mom could. Come on, buddy."

Eden's heart turned over. Would there be a little boy like Sam in her and Jacob's future?

Adriana pulled a bowl of already crushed and strained blackberries from the fridge, then added the goat cheese.

Eden leaned closer. "That looks amazing. What are you doing?"

"This blackberry and cheese blend will be swirled into a thyme-flavored ice cream I churned earlier."

"Sounds awesome." Eden's tummy grumbled.

The back door opened again and Violet sauntered in, looking flushed. Adriana stared at her daughter. "Where were you? I sent you to your room."

Violet shrugged. "I went outside." Her gaze darted to Eden then back to her mom. "I didn't do anything bad."

Adriana set down the spoon she'd been using and faced her child. "What exactly did you do outside?"

"Nothing."

"Violet."

The girl sighed. "I just wanted to see Pansy, okay? It's no big deal."

"It's a very big deal because you disobeyed me. Go to your room right now, and don't come out until I say you may. Do you understand?"

Violet rolled her eyes. "I can too reach the latch." She stomped down the hallway.

Raising a child like her as a single mom must be a challenge every single day.

"Did you know she followed you, Sam?"

The boy cranked the pasta maker handle even harder.

"Sam. You heard me."

"I might've thought I seen her."

"Saw her."

Sam glanced at his mom then back to his job. "Yeah. Saw her. Maybe."

"Sam. Why didn't you tell me?"

"Wasn't sure. Didn't want to be a snitch." Sam turned the handle a few more times. "Are you going to punish me?"

"I'll decide later. Now get the pasta finished, would you? We're nearly ready for dinner."

Eden's memory rocked back in time to Anya's propensity for tattling on her. She'd never felt like she got away with anything. Maybe that was a good thing. Being a parent didn't seem like a walk in the park. But she'd have Jacob, and look how good he'd been with Sierra's kids. Look how good he was about making pasta with Sam.

But then, Adriana hadn't expected to do the job alone, either.

Chapter 23

IT HAD BEEN AN AMAZING evening with friends. Hurricane lanterns, soft music, glasses of mead, laughter, and comfortable conversation on the deck followed the delicious four-course dinner. Jacob felt satisfied in every way — body, soul, and spirit — as he strolled homeward hand-in-hand with Eden.

The moon hadn't risen yet, and few stars were visible between the heavy clouds. A few widely-spaced street lamps offered meager light, but they didn't need more.

Beyond Eden, Rebekah and Wade walked with them. Far away, a coyote howled, and a chorus replied from much nearer. The hairs on the back of Jacob's neck prickled. He knew predators roamed the river bottom. He'd even seen an occasional coyote at a distance in daylight, but these were close.

Eden turned to Wade. "Sounds like dogs, doesn't it?"

"That's what I was thinking."

They all scanned the area by the river, but there was nothing to see in the darkness.

"We've received several calls about packs of feral dogs

lately, but we haven't been able to locate them."

Feral dogs? Jacob tightened his grip on Eden's hand. He hadn't thought of her job being particularly dangerous before. More like finding lost kittens or closing down puppy mills.

"Honey..." Rebekah began.

"Don't worry. They're highly unlikely to attack us, but if they do, I have pepper spray."

Pepper spray. That was good, right?

"Me, too."

Jacob swung to look at Eden in the dim light. "You what?"

She glanced at him. "I carry spray at all times."

"Right now?" Where on earth was she hiding it? She only had a wallet-sized purse dangling from her shoulder. It was so small her keys were clipped to the strap.

"You'll laugh."

"Me? Never." Okay, that wasn't the complete truth.

She lifted her key ring and pointed at a small pink canister hanging from it.

"No way." He choked back a chuckle. "Is there enough in that to subdue a rat?"

"There is." Her voice sounded crisper. "But I do carry big cans when I go on a call. This is just in case."

The howls and barks were nearer now. The coyotes — dogs — whatever they were — had to be in the vacant lots beside the river. They were simply too loud to be any further away.

"Wade..." said Rebekah.

"It's okay, honey." Wade shone a flashlight across the area, catching nothing but shadows.

"No, Wade, listen." She let out a gasp.

Eden stopped in the middle of the road. "Rebekah?"

"I think... I think I'm in labor."

The dogs howled, one keening high above the others.

"Maa."

The faint sound was immediately covered by increased yips and yowls.

Eden jerked away from Jacob. "That's Pansy."

"Can't be." He reached for her hand again but couldn't find it. "She's in her pen. That's in front of us and to the right, not hard left."

"Are you sure?" said Wade. "When did they start? How close together?"

"Pansy!" yelled Eden.

She was wrong, wasn't she? How could the goat be across the street and down by the river? The only time Jacob had ever seen her outside the backyard, she was tethered and Eden was nearby. There was no way... was there?

"I've been feeling weird all evening, but I'm sure this is a contraction. It's the third one, I think."

"Maa."

It was definitely a goat. And definitely not in Eden's backyard.

Wade swung the flashlight wide then at his wife's belly. In the glow, Jacob could make out the other man's face.

"You guys should get on home and get ready to head to the hospital." Eden strode around to the other side of Wade and peered out into the darkness.

"It will likely take a while," Wade said uncertainly. "They say first babies usually do."

Eden turned back to Wade. "Can I borrow your flashlight and pepper spray? Seriously. This is my job. I can handle it from here."

With her own goat and how many dogs? But even Jacob could see the ripples on Rebekah's belly. She needed Wade more right now than Eden did. Than Pansy did. "We've got this." How? He had no clue what he was doing, but Eden did. Surely he could help her.

Rebekah leaned against Wade, eyes closed.

Wade slapped the flashlight into Jacob's hand. A moment later he unclipped the pepper spray from his belt. "Here. Pull the red tab, and it's ready to go. Make sure you're pointing downwind and don't run into it. You have to be within about ten feet, and full in the face."

Jacob nodded, his mouth dry.

"That stuff will make a grizzly think twice. Use it wisely."

"Okay." He only hoped it would be enough.

"Tell Eden I'll call it in. You guys might need backup."

Tell Eden? Where was she? Jacob shone the beam to see her moving into the shadows with her tiny canister out in front of her. He followed her, vaguely aware of Wade swinging Rebekah into his arms and heading down the street.

The beam caught two bright eyes and teeth bared in a fierce growl. This was real. Jacob raised the canister in his other hand. Was it the right direction? Would he blow it into his own face? "Eden?"

"Over here." She was working her way around the beast, who turned to watch her.

Did she really have enough spray in that little thing to do more than annoy the dog? And what of the others? Surely there had been at least two or three from the cacophony of a moment ago. Now all was quiet.

"Maa."

A snarling dog streaked toward Jacob. He pulled the

trigger and took a step back, closing his eyes. The dog whimpered and dropped to the ground, rolling and rubbing its face in the grass.

Jacob's heart pounded in his ears. He whirled to see Eden ejecting her canister on the smaller beast. It went down. He dashed over to her. Surely she didn't have enough spray left if there were more. He pivoted with the beam, watching for more eyes, as his heart rate began to normalize.

"Good job." Eden's voice sounded too loud in the sudden silence. "We don't have long unless Wade comes back with a dart gun. Fifteen minutes, maybe a bit more, before that wears off."

"He said he'd call for backup."

Eden nodded. "So where's Pansy?"

Good question. The last bleat had sounded closer to the river. Jacob scanned the area with the flashlight again, slower this time. A niggling thought poked at him and he pointed it higher. Wasn't Pansy a climber?

He aimed the light up into a tree, catching the gleam of two eyes a dozen feet up. That high? How in the world had she climbed up there? A fallen ponderosa pine leaned against the base, and a narrow branch arched toward Pansy's roost. That branch would never hold Jacob's weight.

"Hey, little girl," crooned Eden. "It's safe to come down now."

Jacob chuckled. "Ever heard of stubborn as a goat? Not likely she'll drop into your arms." He handed the flashlight to Eden then jumped for the lowest limb of the cottonwood. He caught at the rough bark but didn't have quite enough leverage to pull himself up.

"Hoist me?" asked Eden.

Jacob shook his head. "You're wearing a dress." Besides,

she likely wasn't strong enough to carry Pansy back down. He eyed the branch again, gauging the distance and the rough bark. He'd almost caught it the first time. He could do it. He would do it. How much longer did they have before the pepper spray dissipated?

Please, God, give me strength.

He crouched and shot into the air, catching the branch. For a second he swung then he pulled himself up, scraping his chest on the bark. He heaved for breath, looking up.

"Way to go!"

Eden's praise gave him the energy to make his way toward the goat, speaking to her softly. If she spooked or decided to go further up, there wasn't much he could do about it. They called the fire department for cats stuck up trees. Had Fire Station #4 ever rescued a goat?

"Maa." She stretched her nose toward him.

He slid his fingers around her halter and felt her tremble under his touch. "Got her." But he was at least ten feet above Eden's head. It wasn't like he could drop the goat and expect his girlfriend to catch her.

"Now what?"

"I don't know." Jacob rubbed the goat's knobby head, trying to think. He needed both hands to climb back down. Maybe he could rig a sling. He wedged himself in a crook and began to unbutton his shirt with his free hand. "Don't move," he said to the goat. "Don't even twitch." Half the buttons had ripped off when he jumped. He grabbed the band and wrenched downward, listening to the popping buttons and tearing fabric. It couldn't be helped.

Pansy butted his hand, nearly unseating him.

"Whoa, girl!" He managed to keep his balance on the narrow branch as he slid the shirt between her front and rear legs, then draped the sleeves over her back. He'd only have one chance to do this right, or one or both of them was going to fall. Pansy would probably be fine, but he'd be lucky to escape without broken bones.

With his free hand, he looped the sleeves around each other in the beginning of a knot. "Ready?" he called.

"Um. Ready for what?"

"A goat." He grinned into the darkness. "Or, if we're really unlucky, you can catch us both."

"How about we go with Plan A?"

Jacob scratched the goat's head. "Sure. Let's do that one. Ready to fly, Pansy?" He took a deep breath and visualized the moves he'd need to make. Hopefully he wouldn't overbalance before he could grab the branch again.

He grasped both sleeves and lifted Pansy off the branch. Oof. She was heavier than she looked. He wouldn't be able to hold her weight away from his body. He dangled her wiggling body against his leg and shifted down a branch. Then another. Ouch. The rough bark tore at his bare chest. He glanced down at Eden, who'd wisely moved the beam to point lower in the tree.

Pansy squirmed and bleated.

"Hey, girl, it's okay." He rested her on a branch until she stopped scrabbling then managed to get his feet onto a lower limb. So far, so good, but the big drop was yet to come.

"If you can get out on that branch a little, I think I can catch her."

Jacob analyzed Eden's suggestion. "I can try." It better be stronger than it looked, or they'd be back to Plan B. He shifted position, stretching out on the creaking branch, with Pansy dangling free of the foliage in the makeshift sling. His brand new shirt was a goner. Of course, if he broke his neck during the rescue operation, it was a moot point.

"I'm right below you. Whenever you're ready."

The branch creaked. "Here she comes." He reached as far down as he could, arm aching from the weight, then let go.

"Maa!"

"Oomph!"

Then crashing sounds in the bushes. The flashlight fell askew, leaving Jacob staring into the darkness. "You okay?"

"Got her."

"Hope you're both out of the way, because I'm coming down now." Jacob flipped around so he dangled from the branch then flexed his knees and let go. A rock under one foot caused an unbalanced landing as he rolled.

"Are you hurt?" Eden leaned over him, the goat in her arms, shirt sleeves hanging.

Other than raw hands and a burning chest from the bark, fine. Jacob struggled to his feet. Oh, and his throbbing ankle. "Give me that goat. You take the pepper spray in case we need to fight our way out."

Chapter 24

EDEN FOLLOWED JACOB ACROSS THE empty field toward her house with the spray at the ready, keeping an eye on the dogs still groveling in the dirt. They crossed the street. "Here, I'll get the gate for you."

"No need. It's wide open."

She swung the beam forward. "It's what? That Sam! This is all his fault."

"More likely Violet's. She snuck in after him, it sounded like."

True. Sam was trustworthy. His sister? Not so much. "Want to bring Pansy in where we can make sure she isn't injured?"

"Sure."

Eden slammed the gate, and the latch held. She growled. Must have been Violet. That kid. Just wait until Eden gave her what for.

Jacob knelt on the floor inside and set Pansy down. His shirt fell away, smeared in blood. Pansy trotted over to Licorice with no signs of having been bitten or broken.

Eden looked up at Jacob. Twigs were caught in his

tousled hair, and a scratch down his cheek oozed blood. His bare chest had been scraped raw.

No. Eden surged to her feet and closed the gap. "Jacob. Are you okay?"

He raised his hands as though to forestall her, bloodied palms out.

He'd done this for Pansy. For her, Eden. "Thank you." Her gaze caught on his for a long moment, and she stepped closer.

"Let me wash up." He looked down at his chest. "Just scratches. I'm fine. Really." He sidestepped her and headed into the main floor washroom, shutting the door behind him.

He'd be out in a minute, and she'd give him a thanksgiving befitting his actions. Eden scooped up the goat, cradling her against her chest. "Come on. Out to your pen." She carried Pansy out the back door and across the yard then added a small measure of grain to the feeding tray and checked the watering system before closing the gate behind her.

There was no click. Eden frowned. Pushed the gate and pulled it tight again. Still no click. Oh, no. Memory trickled in. Pansy had been in the backyard a few times when Eden was sure she'd been locked in her pen. She'd kept meaning to have a closer look at that latch but never had.

Pansy's escape was her fault. Good thing she hadn't phoned the Diaz residence and given Violet a piece of her mind. She could blame no one else for the escapade that had two dogs suffering from pepper spray and turned Jacob into a bloodied mess. She could only blame herself.

Eden covered her face with both hands and sank to the ground, her back against the fence. She wasn't responsible enough to own livestock.

The back door opened and closed. Jacob. How could she even face him, knowing it was all her fault?

"Eden? You out here?"

She wasn't worthy of him. How could he even love her? He was so meticulous. He did everything right the first time. Tears dribbled down her cheeks, and she bit her lip to keep from crying out.

His footsteps sounded on the porch steps.

Maybe he wouldn't see her. The yard was dark, after all.

He tripped over the bucket in the middle of the yard, sending it clattering toward her. He mumbled something she couldn't be sure of. "Eden! Where are you?"

It was no good hiding. He was going to hurt himself hunting her down in the dark, and she hadn't missed the fact that he'd been limping slightly, even before the bucket. "Here."

In seconds he was in front of her, reaching both hands toward hers. Before she could remind herself not to, she grasped them and allowed him to pull her upright and into his embrace. She rested her cheek against his chest. A few hairs tickled her face and she pulled away.

"It's okay." He pressed her face gently against his skin.

How could it be fine? He'd ruined his shirt for her goat and stood, bare-chested, holding her in darkness only broken by rectangles of light coming from the windows.

His thumb stroked her face as his cheek rested against her hair. "Are you crying? Why the tears, sweetheart? She's okay."

"It's not Pansy." She hiccupped and pressed her hand against his chest to push away. "It's me."

Jacob's hands held her firmly against him. "What's you?"

"It's my fault."

"Violet—"

"No, Jacob. The latch on Pansy's pen isn't catching. I knew it wasn't working right, but I-I forgot to fix it." She held her breath.

He said nothing for a few seconds, his hands running the length of her back.

"Don't hate me," she whispered.

That caused a reaction where nothing else had. "Hate you? I could never."

"But—"

"Eden." One hand caressed her jaw, tipping her face toward his. He covered her mouth with his, kissing her gently but thoroughly. "I love you."

She pushed him away. "But you don't understand. It's my fault she got out. My fault you climbed a tree in your good clothes and ruined your shirt and got all scratched up. My fault—"

"Eden."

Her lips trembled, and she blinked at the welling tears. "What?"

"How about the yard gate? Is that latch broken, too?"

Her mind blanked for a second. "No? I don't think so?"

"Do you ever leave it open?"

Eden shook her head against his chest, and his arms tightened.

"So we're back to Violet."

Realization dawned. Only half her fault. The important half, but still. "Maybe."

"Sweetheart, I'm going to go get a headlamp and my drill, okay? I'll see if I can't fix that latch for you right now. Then you can sleep without worrying she'll get out again."

"I can do it myself. I just have to find my screwdriver."

Jacob chuckled. “I’ve seen your little pink tools, remember? I’ll fix it.” He ran his fingers through her hair, his thumbs caressing her temples. “Be right back.”

She wrapped both arms around herself at the sudden chill as he moved away.

Eden didn’t deserve him. She knew, even if he didn’t, that it would all have been her fault if something happened to him. Just like with her parents and sisters.

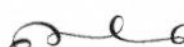

Jacob waited at the park near Eden’s office Monday afternoon as he usually did, but she didn’t come. He glanced at his watch and frowned. Wouldn’t she have let him know if she had to work overtime? He pulled out his phone and sent her a text.

You coming? I’m at the park.

A moment later his phone beeped with her reply. Sorry.

That told him nothing, but it didn’t sound good. Where are you?

Home.

He strode back to his car and sat in the driver’s seat for a moment, wracking his brain for clues he might have missed. She’d been distraught last night, blaming herself for the situation with Pansy. When he’d returned wearing a T-shirt and toting his tools, she’d already gone inside and turned out the lights. He’d fixed the latch — an easy enough task — and returned home to regale Logan with all his housemate had missed while driving Linnea home.

Then he’d spent a near sleepless night between visions of the whimpering dogs, the pain from the rough bark, and the memory of holding Eden close, knowing he'd finally overcome his aversion to her lifestyle.

Now what? Jacob started the car, drove down into Bridgeview, and parked in his own driveway. He jumped over the rosebushes to the protestation of his ankle and knocked on her front door.

A moment later she opened it a crack. Her face was blotchy from tears.

His heart pierced. Had the goat been injured in some way he hadn't noticed? "Eden?"

Her gaze flicked to his face then away. "I'll call you later." She sniffled.

Jacob wedged his foot in the doorway. "Please, sweetheart. What's wrong?"

She shook her head, and the pressure increased on his foot. Good thing he was wearing actual shoes, not sandals.

"Is it Pansy? Did the latch break again?" His brain scrambled. What else could be wrong? They'd had such a good evening before the trauma started. But hadn't he ended it by being her knight errant?

"She's fine."

Jacob reached through the narrow gap and touched the side of Eden's face. "But you're not."

Eden bit her lip, not meeting his gaze.

"Tell me." For the life of him, he couldn't think what he'd done to disturb her so badly. "Please."

"It's no use, Jacob. I'm such a screw-up."

Easy answer there. "No, you're not."

"You don't even know."

"Try me." He lifted her chin through the narrow gap, not that it helped. "Please don't shut me out."

"I make a mess of everything I touch. I don't pay attention to detail. You can't trust me."

"Eden. Please let me in." Any other day he'd ask her to walk down by the river with him, but he wasn't ready to face the spot where everything had happened. "Please."

She looked at him, eyes dull. "Okay."

Jacob resisted the impulse to rub his foot once the pressure was removed. Instead, he followed her into the living room.

Eden grabbed Licorice and sat down on her exercise ball, burying her face in the cat's fur.

That was a clear enough message. "Can I get you a drink of water? Or do you have iced tea in the fridge?"

"Whatever."

He eyed her uncertainly then went past the table and into the kitchen. He found a couple of clean glasses and filled them with iced tea, but there were no ice cubes in the top freezer. Not a big deal. He returned to the living room and set one of the glasses on the stand beside her. His mom would have flipped out that he hadn't set a coaster down first, but he already knew Eden didn't care about such things. Her furniture was old. Stained and scuffed. Jacob took a seat on the sofa, sipped his iced tea, and waited.

"Eden?" he asked softly after a long silence.

"It's always my fault." Her hand clenched over her tattoo.

Jacob barely heard her muffled words. Somehow this seemed bigger than the previous evening. *Lord, give me wisdom.*

"I killed my parents. My sisters."

His gut lurched. "You what?" He tried to envision her holding them at gunpoint and failed. He softened his voice. "How did it happen?" Hadn't she said it had been an accident? That their car had gone under a semi?

"I'd been driving with my friends and fueled up the car. I saw the back tire was low, but I didn't know how to add air, so I left it. I forgot to tell Dad."

"They had a blow-out?"

Eden's head twitched in a nod. "At seventy miles per hour." Tears poured down her face. Licorice squirmed in her grip, but she only tightened it. "And then the big truck hit them."

Jacob knelt by her and wrapped his arms around her. "It's not your fault, sweetheart."

She jerked away from him, nearly unbalancing on the ball. "Yes, it is. Don't you see? If I'd remembered to tell Dad, he'd have filled it. They wouldn't have d-died. All of them."

"Eden, listen to me. Your dad was a grown man. He was what, in his forties?"

"Forty-seven," she whispered.

"And you were twenty. The car was his, right? His responsibility. He should have noticed the tire himself. You were barely more than a kid. You are not liable for the fact that he didn't look."

"But—"

Jacob rested his finger across her lips. "Believe me. It was not your fault."

"And then Pansy's gate. And the house is falling apart around me. I don't know how to fix anything, so I put it off. I—"

"Eden." He slid both hands around her face.

Her hands caught on his wrists, and Licorice leaped free.

"Eden. No one person can do everything. You are amazing. Do you hear me? You've done an incredible job upstairs."

"Hailey—"

"Did Hailey strip every piece of wallpaper and scrub the walls and sand the trim and do the painting and choose the fabric and make everything look so fresh and beautiful?" Like you, he wanted to say, but didn't dare. Not yet.

"She helped."

"I know she got you started, but it was you, sweetheart. You worked every night, every weekend, the entire month I was away. You emailed me. Remember?"

Eden bit her lip but met his gaze for the first time since last night.

"No one is good at everything. No one is perfect. You're not." His thumb slid over her lips. "I'm not."

"You are. Look at you. Always together."

"I can do it on the outside, but you, of all people, know the inside of me is very imperfect. I'm sorry, Eden. Sorry for not seeing you for who you are, for thinking my selfish ways were more important than your dream. I've hurt you, and I'm so sorry."

"This isn't about you." She sniffled. "It's about the mess that is me."

"You're wrong. It's not about either of us. It's about what Jesus wants to do in us and through us. He wants to make us more like Him. I've been praying a lot about this since I got home from Mozambique in August. I want to be more like Jesus. Do you?"

She nodded.

"Then let the guilt go. You know you didn't mean harm to them. Haven't you paid enough?" He bent and feathered kisses over her tattoo.

Then he pulled her to standing and wrapped his arms around her. "I love you."

Eden lifted her face to his and kissed him with the same urgency he felt.

Chapter 25

JACOB'S BROTHER-IN-LAW LIFTED the kennel from the backseat. "Hello, Pansy. Ready to meet the father of your kids?"

Eden's face burned. Yeah, this was an entirely normal situation, but it didn't seem like it. Not with her own boyfriend and his sisters and other friends around her. The drive to northern Idaho had been awkward with Pansy's mournful wails filling Jacob's car.

"Want to come along, Eden?"

She waved Keanan away. "No. Not really. If you don't mind."

"No problem. I'll bring her back in a while." He grinned at her, his eyes soft with understanding, before turning to Jacob. "How about you?"

Jacob shook his head quickly. "No thanks."

Chelsea linked her arm through Eden's. "It seems ages since I've seen you. Come on into the house and let's have a nice visit." She glanced at her brother. "You can come, too, Jakey. It's pumpkin day. You know how it is around here. Many hands make light work."

Pansy's cries of distress faded as Keanan bore the kennel away to the barns. Eden reached for Jacob's hand and caught it, pulling him along as they trooped up the steps to the deck of the large straw-bale house that served as the headquarters for Green Acres Farm.

The memories of her time studying animal husbandry here swam over her. Now she wasn't a student, though. It was almost as though she belonged. Jacob did, for sure, whether he admitted it or not. His sisters' families made up two thirds of the farm's permanent inhabitants.

"Eden!" Sierra wiped pumpkin off her hands and came around the end of the peninsula to give her a big hug. Then she embraced Jacob. "Hi, buddy. Welcome."

"Where are the kids?" he asked.

"Up at Allison's house. She and Claire have all of them. Neither of them can barely reach around their bellies to chop pumpkin anyway." Sierra laughed. "So can I hand knives to both of you?"

When Eden had first met Sierra, the other woman had been deeply mourning her inability to conceive. It was good to see her able to smile over her friends' pregnancies.

"I'm happy to help. I love pumpkin." Eden waved hello to the other folks working in the big kitchen.

"Well, you can definitely take a few packages home with you. But you're staying until tomorrow, aren't you? To make sure Boomer has a chance to do his thing?" Chelsea held up both hands. "Don't ask. He arrived here with that name."

"Yes, we're planning on staying over. Adriana is feeding my chickens. Thanks." Eden didn't want to think about what Pansy and Boomer were up to right now, if nature took its course. Things were so much more complicated for humans. What had Hailey taunted her with that day so long ago now?

First comes love, then comes marriage, then comes Eden with a baby carriage.

They had the love part down pat but, for some reason, Jacob wasn't saying anything about the second part, though several weeks had gone by while he patched her roof, commenting on how solar panels could be mounted. While he replaced the soft boards on her back steps. While he peeled the ugly old carpet out of the living room, exposing the same kind of oak floors as had been hidden upstairs.

As for the third part, he'd make an awesome father. She'd seen him in action with his nieces and nephew. She'd seen him cradling Rebekah and Wade's infant daughter with a look of awe on his face.

All in good time. But when?

He stood behind her now, arms encircling her, chin resting on her shoulder as they watched the bustle in the community kitchen.

"Help me package, Eden?" Chelsea held up a measuring cup.

Eden hated to step out of the warmth of Jacob's embrace, but she pushed his hands away and moved over to his sister. "Tell me what to do."

"She's good at that," Jacob said.

Chelsea made a face at him. "Gabe, give my baby brother a job."

Sierra's husband laughed. "Come on, Jake. Wield a knife, if you will."

Jacob walked over to the huge kitchen island and accepted the blade.

Chelsea glanced over her shoulder and shifted closer to Eden, lowering her voice. "Hasn't he proposed yet? Do I need to speak to that boy?"

Eden grinned. “He runs on his own timetable. You of all people should already know that. I’m sure that’s not something new in the last year.”

“But he moved to Spokane in June, and it’s already October. That’s like four months. And a half.”

“He was away for a few weeks of that.” Not that it made a big difference.

The roll of Chelsea’s eyes showed she agreed. “I’m sure you’ll want to get married here at Green Acres. We’re already booking up for next summer.”

“I, uh...”

“There are still lots of open weekends,” Chelsea assured her. “But you guys shouldn’t wait too long to set a date.”

“I have a home church.”

Chelsea waved her hand. “I know. It’s fun to have a wedding someplace a bit special, though.”

“Well, uh...” What did she say? Eden wiped the mouths of the quart jars and screwed on the lids. “You guys don’t freeze them in bags?”

“We try not to buy plastic. We own an awful lot of jars around here.”

“I bet.” Eden’s mind scrambled for ways to keep the conversation away from her non-engagement. “Do you know if you’re having a boy or a girl?”

Chelsea’s hand rested on her stomach for a few seconds. “We want it to be a surprise. But I felt the baby move for the first time a few days ago. It was the most amazing sensation ever.” And she launched into stories of preparation for their coming little one.

He was somewhat accustomed to the melee at Green Acres, but Eden had that deer-in-the-headlights look. After the delicious — and very loud — communal dinner, Jacob slipped his hand around hers. “Want to go for a walk?” he whispered.

“Yes!” She surged to her feet.

He chuckled and followed her toward the door.

“Don’t forget your jackets. It’s crisp out there.”

Jacob grinned, shaking his head at Chelsea. “We won’t forget. Mom.”

“Well, it’s probably colder here than in Spokane.”

“Because this is the North Pole?” He reached for Eden’s fleece jacket and held it while she slid her arms into the sleeves. Then he grabbed his own.

“Jakey, you should—”

He held his finger to his lips and lowered a gaze at his sister.

She glanced at Eden then back at him. “Sorry.”

“Apology accepted.” He nudged Eden through the door with his hand on her back, then shut them out into the frosty air.

“It’s all a little much,” she murmured, sliding her arm around his waist.

Jacob was only too happy to tuck her close by his side as they meandered down the driveway in the dusk. They passed the school building and turned onto the forestry road before stopping to look back. “This is such a special place to me,” he mused. “You too?”

Why the frown on her face? “I have fond memories of studying here.”

That was an odd answer. He turned her toward him. “City girl,” he murmured and kissed her lips.

"Anything wrong with that?" she whispered.

"Not a thing. I'm kind of a city boy myself." He feathered kisses from her temple to her jawline, and she quivered in his arms. "Doesn't stop me from appreciating what they've done here. Are doing."

"Me either." She turned her face, and her breath warmed the skin below his ear.

"I love you."

"I love you, too," she breathed against his lips.

Her deep kiss was sweet to his mouth. The moment had come. He'd hoped for it. Planned for it. He tried to pull back. To find words.

Eden wasn't ready to let him go. "Jacob." Both her hands cradled his face and held it in place for proper kissing. Not that he really wanted to get away.

At last she released him enough that he could catch his breath. He slid his hands down her arms and caught her hands as he took half a step back. Her gorgeous blue eyes looked directly into his, and it was all he could do not to gather her close once again. Instead, he disengaged one hand and fumbled around in his jacket pocket.

Jacob dropped to one knee in the middle of the dirt road and held out a navy velvet box. "Eden Andrusek, I love you more than I could ever have imagined. The thought of a life without you by my side seems like a world without sunshine. Will you marry me?"

She reached out and touched the velvet box with a fingertip then pulled away, her eyes wide. Her other hand covered her mouth.

What kind of answer was that? "Eden, please. Please say yes."

"Jacob, I..."

Were those tears on her cheeks? "Eden, please?"

"I can hardly believe it!"

"You are everything to me. My paradise. You are the match to my soul's deepest need."

Slowly she knelt in front of him and grasped his hands in both of hers. "Jacob, if you really want me, then yes. Yes, I'll marry you."

"I want you more than I can express." He leaned forward and kissed the tears from her cheeks. "Here. Don't you want to see what I have for you?"

"Yes. But it's nothing compared to your love. Nothing."

He tilted the lid on the little box. "It's a symbol of my promise to you."

She gasped, covering her mouth with both hands as she stared at the glistening diamonds in their custom setting. "It's gorgeous. Where did you ever find it?"

Jacob tugged her left hand toward him and slipped the ring onto her finger. Then he stood — oh, his cramping knees — and helped her up.

Eden turned her hand, and the ring glinted in the beam of the nearby yard light. "I've never seen anything like this. Ever. It's amazing."

"Keanan's mom made it just for you. She's a talented and award-winning designer in Portland."

"Keanan's mom? When did you order it?"

"Six weeks ago. I called her the day after Adriana's dinner party." Safer to say that than remind her of the day Pansy met the feral dogs.

"So everyone in that house knows?" Her luminous eyes met his.

Jacob shook his head. "They have no idea. Fern sent it to me FedEx. It came Thursday. I was just waiting for the right moment to offer it to you. I wanted to ask you on the drive here, but Pansy…" He grimaced. "She just didn't provide the ambience I was looking for."

Her hands slid around his neck and up into his hair, and he gladly pulled her tight against him. He covered her mouth with his, claiming his bride.

"When do you want to get married?" he asked at last.

"I don't know. Spring, maybe? But I do know where."

"Oh? Here at Green Acres?"

She shook her head. "Bridgeview Bible Church, with Pastor Tomas doing the honors. Do you mind?"

He could feel his eyes crinkling as he smiled down at her. "That sounds perfect. Why would I mind?"

"Chelsea seemed to think—" Eden bit off her words.

Jacob shook his head. "What did my sister say this time?"

"She seemed to think I'd want to get married here. But it's not my home. My home is in Bridgeview."

"So is mine." Jacob kissed her nose. "My home is where you are. Now and for always."

Chapter 26

"WOW, THIS PLACE LOOKS AMAZING." Eden looked around the gleaming community center kitchen.

Kass looked up with a grin. "I know! It's like it's not even the same place. So many donations and so much volunteer labor went into this. I can hardly believe it looks so coordinated for all that."

Stainless steel countertops, backsplashes and industrial appliances lined the aging brick walls. Just below the open-beamed ceiling hung a row of colorful framed paintings of various fruits and vegetables by Violet's class at school.

"When are your batch cooking classes starting?" Eden set the box she'd been carrying on the low bench at the back door then began lifting out pumpkin pies. She'd baked eight for the community center's grand opening. Oh, look. Hailey had brought miniature cinnamon rolls. No one would notice if Eden snitched a little one, right? She'd have to remember to ask Hailey for some for the wedding.

"After Christmas. Are you going to join?"

"You bet I am. I can barely keep myself organized. I need to learn to do better before there's two of us."

"You do know that whole thing where the woman does all the housework while the guy reads the paper is so last millennium. Right up there with eighties' wallpaper."

Eden chuckled. "I hear you. The problem is that Jacob's a better cook than I am, and that's a blow to my self esteem."

Kass grinned. "I'm so happy for you. And thank you for asking me to be your bridesmaid. I'm honored."

"You know I had to ask Hailey for maid-of-honor. We go way back."

"Oh, I am perfectly fine with that. And Jacob has asked Logan to be his best man, right? Who are you pairing me with?"

"Wouldn't you like to know?" Eden chuckled.

"Um, yeah, I kind of would."

"A friend of his from Portland. I haven't even met him yet."

"Well, hopefully he's good for a couple of evenings of fun."

"I'm sure."

"Are you girls gabbing in there?" Marietta stood in the door way to the main hall, swathed in a huge white apron. "The table isn't setting itself, you know."

"We know, Marietta." Kass winked at Eden then turned back to the row of serving dishes spread down the long island.

"Let me see that rock." Marietta pointed toward Eden's ring.

Eden held out her hand and allowed the older woman turn it this way and that.

"Humph. Roberto could have given you a bigger one."

"It's not about the size, Marietta. I love Jacob, and he loves me."

"So long as he doesn't take you away from Bridgeview. Your family has been in that house a lot of years, and I'd hate to see you traipse off somewhere else."

"We're in the midst of renovating the house. He's planning to mount solar panels on the roof and one of those Tesla packs on the wall of the laundry room. You've seen the one in the hall?" Eden pointed back the way Marietta had come.

"I saw it." Marietta narrowed her gaze up at the light fixtures. "Is it my imagination, or are the lights a little dimmer than they were with the power company?"

"It's your imagination." Eden laughed to hear Kass saying the words along with her.

"Well, I hope it's dependable." Marietta picked up two salad bowls. "When you girls are quite done chatting, how about bringing out the food?"

"Yes, Marietta. We're on it." Kass's gaze slid past Eden. "Or at least I am. Eden, looks like you have company."

Eden turned to the doorway to see Jacob beckoning her. She wiped her suddenly clammy hands on her dark-wash jeans. "Here goes nothing," she whispered to Kass.

"What are you forgetting?" Marietta blocked her pathway.

"Oops, let me take something out." Eden picked up a tray of hors d'oeuvres and edged past Marietta.

Jacob took the tray from her and set it on the long table just outside the kitchen. "Come on." He took her hand and towed her through the gathering. Near the big open doors, Jacob stopped beside a middle-aged couple. "Mom, Dad, I'd like you to meet Eden. Eden, my parents."

She wasn't sure what she was expecting, knowing the family swam in money. But the man who took her hand had Jacob's laugh lines around his clear blue eyes. "Welcome to the family, Eden. We've heard so much about you."

"Thank you, Mr. Riehl."

He patted Eden's hand. "We'll have none of that nonsense. My name is Tim." He slid his arm around a slim woman dressed in gray slacks and a moss green sweater. "And this is Sandra."

"Pleased to meet you both."

"Oh, come here." Sandra stretched toward Eden with both hands. "Let's not stand on formality. We've heard all about you from Chelsea and Sierra, and even Lilly and Sophie." She flashed a smile at her son. "Jacob might even have mentioned you a time or two."

Eden stepped into the warm embrace of Jacob's mother.

"I'm so glad Jacob invited us to this event. We've been looking for an excuse to spend a weekend in Spokane with both of you."

"Thanks. I've been looking forward to it, too." Oh, if only she could introduce Jacob to her own parents. What would Anya and Indigo have thought of him? She could imagine them hassling him mercilessly. Tag-teaming him.

"Jacob tells us your parents are gone. We won't try to take their place. No one ever can. But we want you to know that we think of you as one of our own. You set the boundaries, and we'll do our best."

Eden dashed the tears away with a swipe of her hand. She'd been alone for so long. The thought of having parents again — sisters again — still overwhelmed her. "Thank you. You have no idea what that means to me."

"You sweet girl. I can see why Jacob says the sun rises and sets upon you."

He said that? She glanced at Jacob and caught the look of love and pride on his face. He slid his arm around her and tucked her against his side. "She's the secret of my sunbeams, and will be all my life." He dropped a kiss to her lips, right there in front of his parents. In front of all their neighbors.

Pastor Tomas whistled for attention, and the room quieted. "We are gathered here together—" he winked at Eden and Jacob "—to dedicate this lovely heritage building as the center of our Bridgeview community. Smell that food? That's what you and your neighbors grew and cooked for tonight's feast, the first of many in this space. Let us give thanks to the One who provides sunshine and rain."

Leaning against Jacob's strong arm, Eden bowed her head. She had so much to be thankful for.

Dear Reader

Do you share my passion for locally grown real food? No, I'm not as fanatical or fixated as many of the characters I write about, but gardening, cooking, and food processing comprise a large part of my non-writing life.

Whether you're new to the concept or a long-time advocate, I invite you to my website and blog at www.valeriecomer.com to explore God's thoughts on the junction of food and faith.

Please sign up for my monthly newsletter while you're there! My gift to all subscribers is *Peppermint Kisses*, a short story set in the Farm Fresh Romance series. Joining my list is the best way to keep tabs on my food/farm life as well as contests, cover reveals, deals, and news about upcoming books. I welcome you!

Enjoy this Book?

Please leave a review at any online retailer or reader site. Letting other readers know what you think about *Secrets of Sunbeams: An Urban Farm Fresh Romance* helps them make a decision and means a lot to me. Thank you!

If you haven't read the original series, the six-book Farm Fresh Romances set on Green Acres Farm, I hope you will. The first story is *Raspberries and Vinegar*.

Keep reading for the first chapter of *Butterflies on Breezes*, the second book in the Urban Farm Fresh Romances.

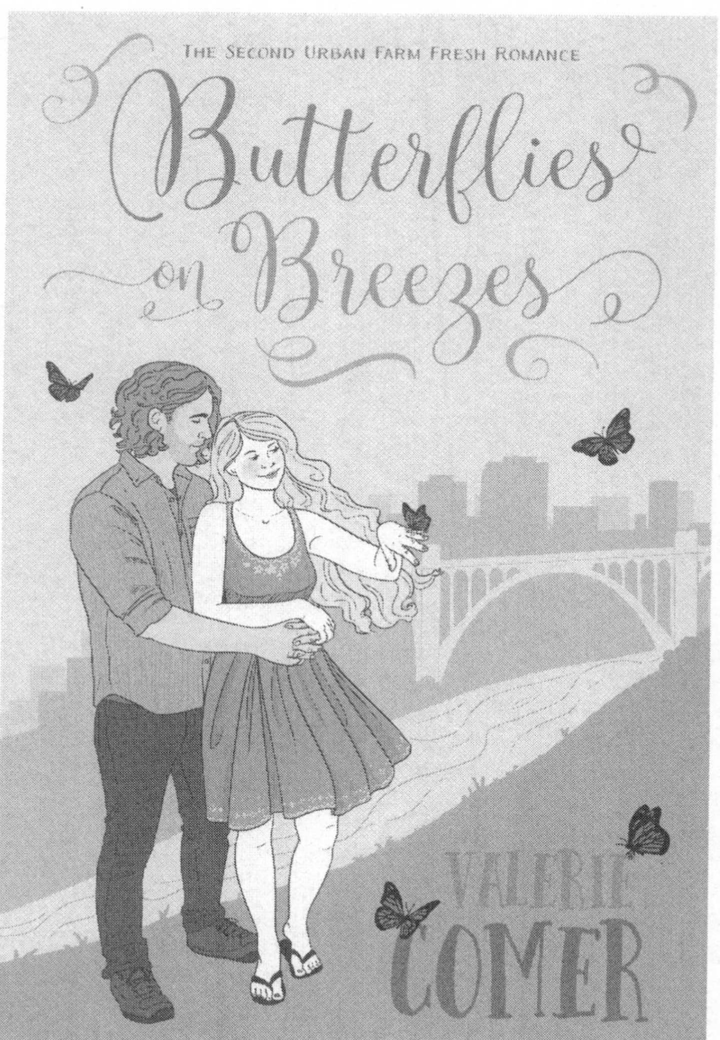
The Second Urban Farm Fresh Romance
Butterflies on Breezes
Valerie Comer

Chapter One

MY GRANDDAUGHTER SEEMS to think you're the right person for this job."

Linnea Ranta quailed under the elderly woman's skeptical look. "I've worked for my dad's landscaping business since I was in high school. I'm sure I can make your dreams a reality." At least, if Marietta Santoro could put those dreams into words or even sketches. So far it had been mostly hand-waving.

"Humph." The woman pointed to the weed-filled lot beyond the wire-mesh fence. Every inch of this side was packed with flowers and vegetables with every tidy row pointing due north. It was no wonder Marietta couldn't stand the sight of the disaster next door. "I want a fence around that. I want raised beds for the neighbors to grow vegetables. I want a watering system and a bench over in that corner under the sycamore."

Maybe Linnea didn't want the job after all. She wasn't a carpenter, and it didn't sound like Marietta had any vision for aesthetics. But it was the first time anyone had approached her directly. Usually clients came to Dad, and he assigned her the jobs he thought were suited to her abilities. This was her chance.

She ducked as a hummingbird zinged to an overhead feeder. Wings flashed as another one chased it away. Hmm. “I see you like birds.”

“Si. Who does not?”

“If you’re keeping the sycamore — which I’m totally a fan of — we could create a bit of a bird habitat in that area. Add some seed-bearing plants and maybe a birdbath.” Linnea snuck a glance at the older woman.

Marietta nodded thoughtfully as she stared through the fence. “That is a possibility. The grandchildren would like to watch birds.”

Maybe this was going to work out after all. “I like your ideas, Marietta. Do you need me to find a builder for the structural parts, or do you have someone in mind?”

The old woman smiled. “Did I not tell you already? That boy who plays the piano at church. He will do it.”

Linnea froze. Logan Dermott? He’d started attending Bridgeview Bible Church about six weeks back and had volunteered to play when the regular pianist was sick. Every time his hands touched the keyboard, the world faded away and Linnea was transported to heavenly realms. He felt the music. He lived the music. In some ways, he *was* the music.

And she’d never missed a Sunday since, just in case he was playing.

“You’ll be in charge, if you take this on. It will be up to you to tell him where to put sixteen four-by-twelve-foot raised beds. There’s a slope...” Marietta scrunched her face thoughtfully. “Well, you figure it out. When you come up with a cost list, please show it to Raimondo, and he will give approval or offer suggestions.”

In charge? Tell Logan what to do? Linnea gulped. Answering to Marietta's son Ray was nothing compared to spending time with Logan Dermott for weeks to come. She tried to imagine giving him orders. Her hands turned clammy. Maybe she should turn Marietta down. Tell her she was too busy. She'd been asked to volunteer, and this was a mighty big job. But it would be worth it if Marietta would give her a good recommendation at the other end.

"Sounds good."

Had that been her voice? Linnea's innards quailed. No, she should have declined, not agreed. Still, Logan Dermott? But what if he already had a girlfriend? Oh, there was no one in Spokane or surely she'd have come to church with him, but maybe somewhere else. A guy like him, so good-looking, confident, and talented, must have women hanging onto him wherever he went.

"He should be here any minute." Marietta checked her watch, clucking impatiently. "He is late."

Linnea took a shuddering deep breath. There wouldn't be time to brace herself for this meeting unless she hurried away right now. But what would that gain? Nothing. She'd agreed to work with him, and it would only prolong her suffering if she put off their first meeting. She wiped her hands down her denim capris.

Cheerful whistling came from behind her.

She whirled to see Logan Dermott rounding the corner of Marietta's white stucco home, wearing faded jeans threadbare in one knee. A white T-shirt, looking a little the worse for wear, stretched over his muscular torso. Tousled hair skimmed his shoulders and he hadn't shaved for several days by the look of the scruff on his chin.

Linnea swallowed hard. He looked amazing in dark

wash jeans and a button-down shirt for church, but a real man who worked for a living was so much more attractive.

"Logan Dermott. You are late." Marietta sounded reproachful.

He grinned at her, a dimple flashing in his right cheek. "I beg your pardon." He took the old woman's hand and kissed it as he bowed over it. Then his gaze rested on Linnea. "I have not had the pleasure of meeting this lovely lady. Where have you been hiding her, Marietta? Is she another of your granddaughters?"

Oh, he was good.

"Not my granddaughter, no." Marietta patted his face. "This is Linnea Ranta from over on Riverside Avenue. She works with her father in his landscaping business. She is going to oversee the community garden project next door. Linnea, this is Logan. He is new to Bridgeview."

His smile widened as he slowly looked Linnea over and finally met her gaze again. "It is my pleasure to meet you, but to work with you on this garden?" He clasped her hand in both of his. "I am looking forward to every moment."

"I, um, it's nice to meet you, too." Somehow she got the words past her lips. His hands were warm and callused. Both his thumbs caressed hers. He was way over the top in his intensity, but somehow it didn't seem too much. Not when warmth that had nothing to do with the July sunshine radiated through her body.

She tugged her hand free. A cloud came over the sun, though there wasn't a single one in the brilliant blue sky, reflected in his twinkling eyes.

"Linnea is as talented as she is *bella*," Marietta said, resting her hand on Logan's arm. "I think I have made a good choice with the two of you."

The smug smile on the old woman's face did nothing to reassure Linnea. Was she really wanting a garden created, or was she playing matchmaker? Because a self-assured man like Logan wouldn't take something like that sitting down. He'd make his own choices, and it wouldn't likely be someone like Linnea. She'd been a shadowed hosta all her life and, though she longed for the light, he'd be looking for a showy flower that danced in the sunshine.

What was Marietta up to? The neighborhood matriarch looked like she'd swallowed the proverbial canary. So she was setting them up for more than a garden. Did she do this kind of thing often? Well, there was no harm done in playing along for now. Linnea looked a little shy, but she was certainly pretty enough. Plus he'd already agreed to help with the garden. It didn't much matter with whom he worked. A bit of flirting wouldn't go amiss.

Logan turned to Marietta. "How do you expect me to get any work done with such a beautiful woman nearby? I'm sure I'll be too distracted."

"There is no rush. It is too late to grow most things yet this summer. We only need to be ready for springtime."

He didn't miss the sharp look Linnea gave Marietta. So he wasn't the only one noticing. Interesting.

"Would you like to walk around the space with us?" Logan gestured to the gate leading through the wire-mesh fence to the unkempt lot next door. "Perhaps give some ideas as to what you'd like to see where?"

Marietta set her hand over her heart. "No, I am tired.

You two go ahead. When you've had a chance to draw some preliminary plans, bring them to me. If my son Raimondo approves, you may present him with a list of materials to purchase."

Logan had met Ray Santoro several times around the neighborhood and at church. The man would definitely be easier to deal with than his eccentric mother. "Sounds good." He turned to Linnea. "Do you have a few minutes now, or shall we set another time to do a walk about?"

Linnea's gaze flicked to his then away. "We could take a few minutes now if you have time."

"Always time for a beautiful woman." He took Linnea's arm and nodded at Marietta. "We'll get back to you later."

Marietta touched her thumb and forefinger together as she smiled. "I will wait in eagerness."

Logan steered Linnea toward the gate and ushered her into the other yard. "Marietta is something else, isn't she," he murmured, angling his head close to hers. "She wants more than a garden."

Linnea's long blond hair brushed against his arm like a rippling breeze as she turned to glance at him. "I don't have to do this. She can find someone else."

She wasn't his usual type being so near his own height and really quite thin. Her white tank top showed off minimal assets, and now he knew where the term skinny jeans had come from. But the face was definitely pretty, and the blue eyes seemed shadowed with something deeper.

"Or we can play along for now. I am definitely in need of something to do, and working with you to transform this space sounds like a terrific way to spend time." Logan grinned. "Who knows? Maybe her fond wishes will come true."

Was that a pink flush shooting across her face? Interesting. He'd have to be careful. Hurting someone was never part of the package.

Linnea pulled away from his touch and strode to the middle of the lot. "She wants sixteen four-by-twelve-foot raised beds, so those will take up a good half of the area. We'll need to do some terracing, though."

He wandered closer, careful to leave some distance between them. "It's not much of a slope. I'm sure we can manage that."

"We'll need paths between them wide enough for a wheelbarrow." She spread her hands apart. "So, a good three feet. Maybe four."

Logan nodded. "Makes sense."

"I'm not sure what she's told you. I know she wants you to construct a picket fence around to keep the neighborhood dogs out."

"And the raised beds themselves, as well as some benches and a gazebo."

"A gazebo? She didn't mention that to me."

"I think she wants to keep me busy for a while." He grinned wryly.

Linnea shot him an unreadable glance.

"But I'm in it for whatever you need. I can help with the terracing. Digging. Laying sod. Whatever you need help with." Transforming ninety-thousand square feet would take a lot of digging. A lot of time.

And he could think of worse ways to spend it, especially since his housemate was dating the girl next door and seemed to never be home.

"I can bring in Dad's Bobcat to do the heavy lifting."

His eyebrows rose. "You can drive a Bobcat?"

"And why not?" Her fists landed on her narrow hips. "I've been working with my dad since I was in high school. This isn't the first time I've encountered real work."

Logan could see definition in those biceps, small as they were. "Okay, I believe you." He raised both hands. "You're the boss. I'm just the serf, here to do your bidding. Whatever you want done, I am at your command."

Her face reddened again. It was going to be far too easy to fluster this woman, but walking on eggshells belied his very personality.

Butterflies on Breezes
is available where you purchased
Secrets of Sunbeams

Author Biography

Valerie Comer lives where food meets faith in her real life, her fiction, and on her blog and website. She and her husband of over 35 years farm, garden, and keep bees on a small farm in Western Canada, where they grow and preserve much of their own food.

Valerie has always been interested in real food from scratch, but her conviction has increased dramatically since God blessed her with three delightful granddaughters. In this world of rampant disease and pollution, she is compelled to do what she can to make these little girls' lives the best she can. She helps supply healthy food — local food, organic food, seasonal food — to grow strong bodies and minds.

Valerie is a USA Today bestselling author and a two-time Word Award winner. She has been called "a stellar storyteller" as she injects experience laced with humor into her green clean romances.

To find out more, visit her website at www.valeriecomer.com, where you can read her blog, explore her many links, and sign up for her email newsletter to download the free short story: *Peppermint Kisses: A (short) Farm Fresh Romance 2.5*. You can also use this QR code to access the newsletter sign-up.

Made in the USA
Lexington, KY
16 July 2016